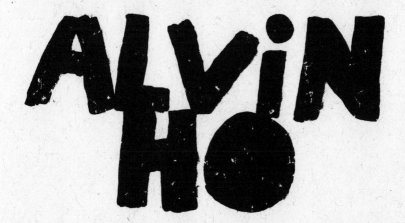

ALVIN HO

ALLErGiC To BiRTHDAY PARTiES, SCiENCE PRoJECTS, AND oTHER MAN-MADE CATASTRoPHES

ALVIN HO

ALLERGIC TO BIRTHDAY PARTIES, SCIENCE PROJECTS, AND OTHER MAN-MADE CATASTROPHES

BY Lenore LOOK   PICTURES BY LeUyen Pham

schwartz & wade books · new york

All rights reserved. Published in the United States by Schwartz & Wade Books, an imprint of Random House Children's Books, a division of Random House, Inc., New York.

Schwartz & Wade Books and the colophon are trademarks of Random House, Inc.

Visit us on the Web! www.randomhouse.com/kids

Educators and librarians, for a variety of teaching tools, visit us at www.randomhouse.com/teachers

Library of Congress Cataloging-in-Publication Data
Look, Lenore.
Alvin Ho : allergic to birthday parties, science projects, and other man-made
catastrophes / Lenore Look ; [illustrations by LeUyen Pham]. — 1st ed.
p. cm.
Summary: When second-grader Alvin Ho is invited to a birthday party
given by a girl, his fear of everything causes him to dread going.
ISBN 978-0-375-86335-6 (trade) — ISBN 978-0-375-96335-3 (glb) —
ISBN 978-0-375-89498-5 (e-book)
[1. Fear—Fiction. 2. Self-confidence—Fiction. 3. Parties—Fiction. 4. Interpersonal
relations—Fiction. 5. Schools—Fiction. 6. Chinese Americans—Fiction.
7. Concord (Mass.)—Fiction.] I. Pham, LeUyen, ill. II. Title.
PZ7.L8682Aq 2010
[Fic]—dc22
2009050622

The text of this book is set in Adobe Caslon.
The illustrations are rendered in ink.
Book design by Rachael Cole

Printed in the United States of America

10 9 8 7 6 5 4 3 2 1

First Edition

This book belongs to
Charity Chen,
who had no fear of science projects
or birthday parties
ever.
—L.L.

To the great Uncle Rob, who always buys the BEST gifts!
—L.P.

AUTHOR'S ACKNOWLEDGMENTS

"Be true to your word and your work and your friend."
        —John Boyle O'Reilly, "Rules of the Road,"
            Life of John Boyle O'Reilly, 1891

With heartfelt thanks to:
Anibelly Kelley, for taking Alvin and the whole gang to
Vermont with her.

LeUyen Pham, for drawing all the Phamtastatic pictures!

Sophie Fisher, for her research and photos of the you-know-
what at Orchard House, and

Vivian Low Fisher, for driving her there.

All the fabulous kids in my life who are always giving me lots of
story ideas for Alvin, whether or not they know it, including
Sophie, Sam, Bell, Buddy, Shepherd, Kevin and Andrew.

CHAPTER ONE
One Foot in the Grave

my name is Alvin Ho. I was born scared, and I am still scared. I never thought I'd live to see myself in another book, on account I could've very well died camping in that last one. The good news is that I had the secret powers of my Batman ring and my rolls of toilet paper with me. They saved my life.

The bad news is, there's still a lot of other things that could kill me, just like that:

Giant octopus.

Giant trees.

Giant anything.

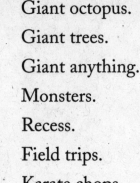

Monsters.

Recess.

Field trips.

Karate chops.

Pork chops (if they're not well-done).

Chopsticks (if you fall on them).

The kiss of death.

The safest place for me to be is home, if you don't count the fact that my home is in Concord, Massachusetts, which is hard to spell. It's where the American Revolutionary War began, with lots of explosions and bad language and dead bodies all over the place. There aren't any dead bodies out there anymore, but there sure are a lot of creepy dead authors who still live inside their homes, giving tours, instead of lying around at the Sleepy Hollow Cemetery where they belong. Normally, this isn't a big problem, like setting fire to the woods, it's just an average problem, like having the match.

But today was not normal.

When I got to school this morning—surprise, surprise—we hopped right back on the bus after A&A (attendance and announcements).

"Hey, it's time for handwriting class!" I screamed as the bus rolled down the street, away from school. I love handwriting class.

"Hooray, no handwriting today!" yelled Pinky, whose handwriting looks like hair floating in the ocean. "Yippie!"

"Did you forget?" asked Flea, who was sitting next to me. "It's our field trip day." Flea's a girl. Otherwise, she's okay. She wears a patch over a genuine pirate eye, and one of her legs is longer than the other, like a real peg leg. But she's still a girl.

Field trip? What field trip?

"I've been looking forward to this all week!" shrieked Esha.

"Me too!" said Sara Jane.

I love field trips. I'm just not good at remembering them.

The wheels on the bus went round and round.

Scooter and Jules's thumbs went up and down in a thumb-wrestling match.

Then their fists went left-hook, right-hook in a boxing match.

Then Nhia, who is a ninja from Cambodia, slipped a head-hold on Pinky, who has the biggest head in the class on account of he's the biggest boy, and Pinky screamed into Nhia's armpit, which made Hobson whack Eli on the head, which made Sam karate-chop Scooter with a loud "Aiyah!", which made our teacher,

Miss P, who was sitting at the front of the bus, turn around and yell, "SIMMER DOWN, BOYS, OR YOU'LL GET A NOTE SENT HOME!" How she knew who was doing what, all the way from the front of the bus and facing the other way, I'll never know. But she's very smart and smells like fresh laundry every day. Maybe she has eyes in the back of her head, just like my mom.

The noise on the bus simmered down.

When mouths close, something else is supposed to open, it's one of the rules of school.

In this case, it was Scooter's lunch box.

Scooter's dad is a cook in a restaurant and Scooter gets restaurant leftovers for lunch. And when Scooter opens his lunch box, people sniff.

It smelled like cold fried chicken. It *was* cold fried chicken!

Heads turned.

Mouths watered.

Scooter's teeth sank into the chicken.

Juice dribbled down his chin.

This made Hobson, who's a little roly-poly, yelp that he was hungry too, and rip open his lunch bag—just as the bus went around Monument Square, which isn't square at all, it's a circle—and something went flying. I think it was raisins. Yes, it was raining raisins!

Then it rained sea-weed crackers! Then potato chips! Then my favorite—Goldfish crackers! Oh, I love field trips!

The noise on the bus got louder and louder.

Miss P was not pleased. She yelled, "IT'S NOT LUNCHTIME YET!" But her voice got swallowed by the noise and you had to read her lips.

And I yelled, "WILL SOMEONE PLEASE TELL ME WHERE WE'RE GOING?" I like field trips, but I don't like surprises.

It was too late anyway, our bus was slowing to a stop—at the mouth of the Old Hill Burying Ground!

And before I knew it, Miss P was marching us up a steep hill of dead people lying in the ground, looking up at the sky.

It was SO CREEEEEPY, I could've died right there!

But I didn't. I clutched my PDK (Personal Disaster Kit), which contains all the things that are useful in a disaster, such as escape routes, garlic, lucky charms, a scary mask (for keeping girls away) and a wishbone for when nothing else works. And I tried to look as alive as possible, and to step lively, but not step on any graves, just in case.

I hopped from stone to stone on the path, following Miss P and the rest of the class, until we were going down the hill in the back of the graveyard to where the path disappeared . . . and some of the oldest and spookiest tombstones were poking out of the grass like black, crooked teeth.

When Miss P finally stopped, she was hardly out of breath, but the rest of us were panting like we had had too much recess. In front of us was the most crooked tooth of all, a black slab that looked like it was about to fall over on its back. On it was a poem:

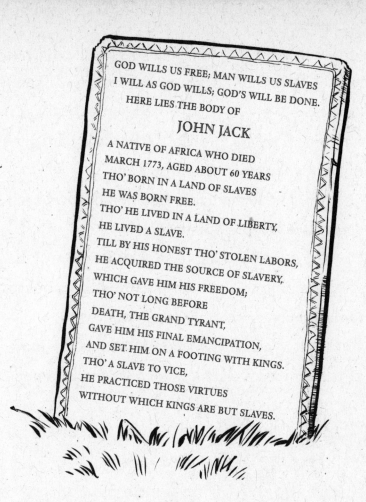

GOD WILLS US FREE; MAN WILLS US SLAVES
I WILL AS GOD WILLS; GOD'S WILL BE DONE.
HERE LIES THE BODY OF

JOHN JACK

A NATIVE OF AFRICA WHO DIED
MARCH 1773, AGED ABOUT 60 YEARS
THO' BORN IN A LAND OF SLAVES
HE WAS BORN FREE.
THO' HE LIVED IN A LAND OF LIBERTY,
HE LIVED A SLAVE.
TILL BY HIS HONEST THO' STOLEN LABORS,
HE ACQUIRED THE SOURCE OF SLAVERY,
WHICH GAVE HIM HIS FREEDOM;
THO' NOT LONG BEFORE
DEATH, THE GRAND TYRANT,
GAVE HIM HIS FINAL EMANCIPATION,
AND SET HIM ON A FOOTING WITH KINGS.
THO' A SLAVE TO VICE,
HE PRACTICED THOSE VIRTUES
WITHOUT WHICH KINGS ARE BUT SLAVES.

It was the most writing I'd ever seen on a tombstone. It looked like an entire book!

"Good morning, boys and girls," said a voice.

I jumped out of my skin! The only voices in a cemetery are dead ones . . . but this one belonged to a man who was hurrying toward us, dressed in old-fashioned clothes, *very* old-fashioned clothes.

"Sorry I'm late," he said. "It's a little hard getting up when you're as old as I am."

Old? He looked like he should have been dead three hundred years ago!

"My name is Ralph Waldo Emerson," he said, stopping to catch his breath at the crooked tombstone.

Ralph Waldo Emerson? What was he doing at the cemetery? He's one of Concord's famous

dead authors who's still living in his house giving tours.

"Normally I just give tours of my house," the
dead author continued. "But you're on the
Abolition Tour today and because of my family's
history in the slave trade, I will be your first
guide."

A hair-raising wind blew through my
shirt.

"You're standing at the grave of one of Concord's earliest slaves," said the pale Mr. Emerson.
"His name was John Jack, and he belonged to a
shoemaker."

Concord had slaves? I could hardly believe
my ears.

"Yes, Concord had plenty of slaves," said the
pale author.

Yikes! Can dead people hear our thoughts?

A big black crow floated above our heads and
cawed, *"Aw, aw, aw."*

"Isn't this cool?" Flea whispered.

Cool? A chill went up my spine.

I shuddered and closed my eyes and went to

my happy place. It's summertime and I'm at the Old North Bridge with my family. My mom thinks we're picnicking and my dad's pointing out the spot on the hillside where the Minutemen were hiding from the Redcoats, but little do they know that fighting is actually breaking out on the bridge between the Redcoats (my big brother, Calvin, and my little sister, Anibelly) and the Minutemen (me and my dog, Lucy). Bang! Bang! Bang! It's the beginning of the American Revolution! Redcoats are dropping dead! Minutemen are dropping dead! There are no slaves anywhere. Only a few tourists, and they run away.

But then my happy place was interrupted. "Slaves were not allowed to fight at North Bridge," said Mr. Emerson.

My eyes fluttered open.

"It was against the law for blacks to join the militia then," said the creepy author. "But they were later allowed to serve in the war."

Aaaaaaqaaaaaaaaaaaack! He *could* read my

thoughts! I wanted to scream. But nothing came out. Goose pimples turned me into a cactus.

I eyed Mr. Ralph Waldo Emerson carefully. He had deep wrinkles and silver hair, just as you would expect a three-hundred-year-old dead body to have.

Then he eyed me.

I gasped.

"My great-grandfather owned a ship which brought in thousands of slaves to Boston," said the dead author. "He helped turn the city into a major slave-trading center. But I believed that slavery is a great evil, so I wrote and spoke out against it.

"Many Concord families hid runaway slaves in their homes," he continued. "They were part of the Underground Railroad, which was not about trains, but about giving runaway slaves places to hide as they made their way to Canada. I will show you a couple of those homes now."

Then he marched us right out of the cemetery. For a dead guy, his legs moved pretty fast!

And boy, was I glad to leave! But then we followed him right up the street and stood on the sidewalk in front of a creepy old house.

"This was the home of Henry Thoreau's jail keeper, Sam Staples," said the dead Mr.  Emerson. "This house had a secret closet, a secret tunnel and a secret cave in the back. After Henry spent a night in jail for refusing to pay his poll tax as a protest against slavery, his jail keeper turned his own house into a station on the Underground Railroad."

"Can we go in?" asked Eli.

"I want to see the secret cave," said Sara Jane.

"Please take us in!" everyone cried, jumping up and down—everyone, that is, except me.

My heart was thumping like crazy. I don't like creepy old houses, especially ones with a *history*.

"I'm afraid we can't go in there," said the dead author. "It's closed for renovations."

He must have heard my thoughts again!

It's a good thing Miss P told us to get back on the bus just then. I was beginning to feel very allergic. If I'd had to stand there one second more, I would've broken out the survival gear in my PDK, and who knows what might have happened next!

Instead, I was safe on the bus again. . . .

Our bus pulled away from the mouth of the cemetery. . . .

Away from the creepy dead author . . .

And rumbled around Monument Square . . .

Then down the street past the shops. It was a very close call.

As I began to swing my feet a little, we stopped.

I looked out the window.

I blinked.

Then my eyes popped out like Ping-Pong balls.

We had stopped in front of a yellow house, where—gasp!—Mr. Emerson stood waving at us! If there's anything I hate about Concord,

Massachusetts, which is hard to spell, it's that the dead are everywhere!

Miss P waved back. Then she herded us off the bus.

"Many of you know the Thoreau-Alcott House," said the eerie Emerson. "Henry's mother rented out rooms, but they also hid runaway slaves here."

"And that's the room where Henry died!" shrieked Jules, pointing at one of the front windows. "My mom told me!"

Everyone turned to look—everyone, that is, but me.

I didn't have to turn.

I was standing right in front of the window.

"Yes, this is the house where Henry Thoreau died," said our dead tour guide. "He was a good friend of mine. . . ."

I didn't hear anything else he said.

I kept my eye on the window.

I clutched my PDK.

I held my breath.

Suddenly, something behind the curtain—moved!

Aaaaaaaaaaaaaaack! I wanted to scream, but I couldn't. My mouth opened, but nothing came out. My hands went up in the air . . . my PDK swung open . . . and out spilled garlic, dental floss, my whistle, extra lunch money, Band-Aids,

a bunch of lucky charms, a scary mask and all my escape routes! It was a genuine personal disaster!

I ran and hopped right back on the bus.

Then everyone else screamed and hopped back on the bus too.

And that was the end of that.

Miss P was not pleased. "ALVIN HO," she yelled from the front of the bus, "PLEASE COME SEE ME WHEN OUR FIELD TRIP IS OVER."

Gulp.

"AND NOW, BOYS AND GIRLS," shouted Miss P, "YOU'RE IN FOR A REAL TREAT—PART TWO."

Part Two?

CHAPTER TWO

Part Two— The Sequel

my brother, calvin, is nine and knows a lot of things. For example, he knows that when they make a scary movie, they always make a sequel. And the sequel, he says, is always scarier than the original.

So when they make a field trip, and it's scary, and there's a Part Two, the best thing to do is to *not go*. But if you're already on your way, then the best you can do is to stay out of sight.

So I flattened.

I folded into Alvin the paper airplane.

Then I drifted up and out the school bus window, where I could ride *above* the bus, but not *in* the bus, where I would be stuck going to Part Two. Being a paper airplane is super-duper!

Soon our big yellow bus pulled up right in front of—Orchard House, Home of the Alcotts.

Lucky for me, I was a paper airplane . . . and not a boy. . . .

"Alvin? Earth to Alvin," said Flea, who was sitting next to me. "We're here, Alvin."

Oooh. Girls are so annoying.

Just like that, I was a boy again.

My throat tightened.

My knees locked.

I clutched my empty PDK and what was left of my lunch to my chest and froze.

I could hardly believe it. If I had known I was going to the Alcott house, I would have gotten malaria.

"Miss P," Flea shouted, "I think Alvin needs the bathroom."

"Alvin?" yelled Miss P from the front of the bus. "Can you hold it? We'll be inside in just a minute."

Laughter rocked the bus.

But it wasn't funny. I couldn't move. And Flea, who likes to be helpful and likes to speak for me at school, was wrong. I didn't need the bathroom. I needed to go home.

How I ever made it off the bus, I'll never know.

How I ever made it up the front walk is a mystery too, but I think we had to use the buddy system and hold hands with someone so that no one would get lost between the bus and the bushes.

So I can't tell you how I finally ended up at the house . . .

Where an owl was hoo-hoo-hooting . . .

And the giant arms of gigantic trees swayed closer and closer . . .

Where the door creaked open . . .

And a voice came out.

"Welcome, boys and girls." It was a lady dressed in old-fashioned clothes—*very* old-fashioned clothes, like the kind Ralph Waldo Emerson wore. "I'm Louisa May Alcott, and I'll be taking you through my home today."

Louisa May Alcott???!!! She died three hundred years ago, as everyone knows! I opened my mouth to scream, but nothing came out. My skin felt like paper. My tongue rolled up like a carpet.

But mysteriously, my feet started moving forward, like everyone else's, and we followed the dead author right through her gift shop and straight into her spooky kitchen.

"When we first moved to Concord, we lived in the house next door," said the dead Louisa May. "I was a young teenager then, and I remember my parents hiding runaway slaves. My father was a good friend of Ralph Waldo Emerson, and we moved from Boston to be close to him."

Louisa May looked around at everyone. Then she looked me smack in the eye. Gasp!

After that, the audio portion of the program went dead.

I didn't hear anything she said in her dining room.

I didn't hear anything she said in her parlor.

I didn't hear anything she said in her dad's study.

In fact, I don't remember those rooms at all, except for a couple of creepy paintings that had eyes that followed you.

"This place gives me the creeps," said Sam.

"Me too," said Nhia.

I said nothing. I'd been to Orchard House once before with my family, and the only thing I remember from that

visit was that I had to be carried out like a corpse.

But the girls weren't scared at all.

"It must have been fun doing plays in the dining room and having your audience in the parlor!" Flea said to Sara Jane.

"Yeah, and to change costumes too!" said Ophelia.

They hurried behind Louisa May up the stairs, but Miss P had to shoo the boys to get us to go up.

Swish, swish, swish, went the dead author's three-hundred-year-old dress.

Creak, creak, creak, went the stairs.

"This is the room where I wrote in my journal and wrote my stories," said Louisa May when we got upstairs. "And this is the desk that I wrote at. My father made it for me."

On her desk was an old-fashioned pen, the kind you dip into ink. It was sitting next to a glass ball for holding ink, but it was empty. There was no ink.

But there sure was a lot of writing on a piece

of paper right in front of it. How did she write all that without any ink? It was very creepy.

My stomach lurched.

My hands slipped on my still-empty PDK.

"And now this is my favorite part of the tour," said the pale Louisa May. "You may sit in my room awhile and write something in your journals."

Miss P beamed. "We've been practicing writing in our journals," she said. "And everyone has been looking forward to doing that here."

We have?

Louisa May pointed to a big, spooky photograph of her dad on the wall. Then she pointed at an owl that her sister had painted on the fireplace. A small owl statue peered from the mantel.

I looked around.

I wondered if Louisa May had died on *that* bed.

I shuddered.

Before I knew it, everyone was sitting on the faded flowery carpet and had pulled out their notebooks and was scratching away at them with their pencils. Everyone, that is, except me. I was standing in the middle of the room, my mouth wide open, my eyes glued to *her*. And I was *stuck*.

"Alvin?" I heard Miss P say. "Did you remember your journal?"

Journal?

"He needs the bathroom," Flea tried to whisper to Miss P. Flea is always trying to be helpful, but whispering isn't one of her talents.

"Oh dear!" said Miss P. "I forgot!"

Laughter rocked the room of the dead.

I didn't need the bathroom. But I couldn't say so. I was all freaked out. And when I'm all freaked out, like whenever I'm in school, I can't talk, I can't grunt, I can't even squeak.

"I'll show him where it is," said the very creepy Louisa May.

I could have peed in my pants! But I didn't. Like I said, I didn't need the bathroom.

"C'mon," she said. "This way." If this were a scary movie of my life, this would be the part where the spooky music gets louder and louder and everything in the room begins to spin, and you would know that I was about to die.

But this wasn't a movie, it was the *real* thing! And mysteriously, my feet were slipping and sliding right out of the room.

Swish, swish, swish, went the three-hundred-year-old dress down the stairs. *Squeak, squeak, squeak,* went

my sneakers after her. We walked back through the same creepy rooms until we got to the gift shop, where—gasp!—we bumped into another Louisa May!

"Hey," said the other Louisa May, who was also wearing a three-hundred-year-old dress.

"Hey yourself," said the first Louisa May.

"How's your group going?" asked the second Louisa May.

"Fine," said Louisa May, "except for this kid who needs the bathroom."

"There's one in every group," said the other.

"It's there in the corner, kid," said the original Louisa May, pointing past the books. "Don't take too long, or your group will leave without you."

The Louisa Mays giggled.

Normally, I love gift shops. But I had no time to love this one. I shot into the bathroom as fast as I could and locked the door. My heart was jumping around like a kangaroo on fire!

I pumped the soap.

I washed my hands.

I checked myself in the mirror.

I flushed the toilet, just in case.

Then I sat on the toilet. I pulled out my pencil and notebook and wrote in my best shaky handwriting:

How to survive a creepy dead author house tour
1. Go to the bathroom.
2. Lock the bathroom.
3. Stay in the bathroom.

I added my new emergency plan to my PDK. But the problem with my PDK was that it was empty. I'd lost everything on the Thoreau-Alcott lawn.

And the problem with being in the bathroom was that it was suffocating. It was a small, enclosed space with a slanted ceiling, like— a coffin!

I didn't feel so good.

I have claustrophobia.

Quickly I pushed back the curtains and looked out the window.

I gasped.

Beneath the trees, there were not two Louisa Mays, but *three* Louisa Mays, and they were all standing around, laughing! One was even smoking! Yikes! Clones!

I knew all about clones. A clone is a copy-cat, but no one can tell it apart from the real thing until the clones take over the world

and it's too late. And as everyone knows, humans and clones cannot peacefully coexist.

I don't remember what happened next. If I were a girl, I might have fainted. But I'm not a girl. I'm a boy. So I just passed out. Then I had a dream. . . . In my dream police sirens were wailing and a fire truck too. It was super-duper! Then a bunch of cop cars screeched to a halt and surrounded Orchard House. "Will the real Louisa May Alcott please come out with your hands up!" a policeman's voice boomed through a megaphone. "You are under arrest to go to the cemetery."

Everything was going just great until . . . *boom, boom, boom!*

"Is someone in there?" a voice yelled. "Open this door, or we're comin' in."

I blinked my eyes open.

I was sprawled in an X on a cold, hard floor.

Where was I?

It didn't feel like home. . . .

It didn't feel like school. . . .

Then through the door I heard *swish, swish, swish*—the sound of three-hundred-year-old skirts.

"AAAAAAAAAAAAAAAAAAAAACK!" My mouth opened to scream, but nothing came out.

Then a HUGE Louisa May, the size of Godzilla, cracked the door off its hinges like a graham cracker from a gingerbread house.

The hairs on my head stuck out like one of GungGung's Chinese calligraphy brushes struck by lightning.

Clones are super-duper strong. They can rip a door from the wall and suck all the air out of the room, just like that.

The good news is that I didn't miss our bus, and Miss P forgot all about busting me.

Whoever said field trips are educational was right. I learned quite a lot today.

Like don't mess with Louisa Mayzilla.

CHAPTER THREE

A Two-Pound Hairball

TGIS. thank god it was Saturday.

On Saturdays, I'm—FIRECRACKER MAN!!!

"Bakbakbakbakbakbak!" I screamed, popping like a string of firecrackers on Chinese New Year. I was zooming around my yard in my Firecracker Man outfit, saving the world and keeping an eye on Lucy and another eye on Anibelly, who was

digging holes in the yard with one of my carved sticks.

"Lalalalalalala," sang Anibelly, who sings whenever she's happy.

If there's anything I love about Anibelly, it's this—she's happy. When you hang out with her, you feel happy too. For a little sister, she's okay. But if there's anything I don't love about Anibelly, it's that she's a girl. And girls are annoying, as everyone knows. She's practically attached to me like a flower to a stem. And it's hard to get away from her when you're the stem. But today I had an idea.

"B-R-B!" I screamed, which is faster to say than Be Right Back! Then I zoomed off, across our neighbor's yard, through the gate and down the street toward the noise coming from Jules's house, which is on the way to everything.

Through the bushes I could see that the gang was there, and everyone was galloping wildly about, hollering war cries that sounded like they were coming right out of King Philip's War. In fact, it *was* King Philip's War! And

King Philip's War, as everyone knows, is the war between settlers and natives that nearly wiped out all of Massachusetts a hundred years before the American Revolution wiped out everyone else. So when the gang isn't playing the American Revolution, they're playing King Philip's War.

"*Wooofwooooff,*" said Lucy, who had followed me. She slipped through a crack in the bushes and into Jules's yard. Lucy always says hello. She's very friendly. And when she's with me, people are friendly to me too. So I slipped through the bushes after her.

"Hey, Alvin!" said Jules.

I tipped my head to one side. That's "hey" in body language.

It's hard to tell if Jules is a boy or a girl, but it didn't matter on account of the fantastic war paint on his or her face! Nhia was wearing a tricorn hat, and Scooter and Sam had on pilgrim hats from last year's Thanksgiving Day parade. Eli was dressed as Abraham Lincoln, who had come to dinner once in Concord, Massachusetts, which is hard to spell. And Abe Lincoln, as everyone knows, can play settlers and Indians without dressing like one if he wants. Pinky, who is very bossy, was wearing a big feather on his head and a blanket around his shoulders. He was the Indian leader, King Philip.

"It's settlers against Indians," called Sam. "We're practicing for Hobson's party."

"You're going, aren't you?" asked Eli.

I shrugged.

"Didn't you get an invitation?" asked Jules.

What invitation?

"Maybe you weren't invited," said Pinky, who speaks for everyone on account of he's the leader of the gang. Besides, Hobson wasn't there.

I shrugged. I don't like birthday parties anyway. They're un- predictable; any- thing can happen. And you have to be on your best behavior the *whole* time. But I did want to play King Philip's War. And I did want to be invited to something with the rest of the gang.

"Do you have settler gear?" Pinky asked.

I shook my head no.

"How 'bout Indian gear?"

I shook my head again.

"No wonder you haven't been invited," said Pinky. "No war paint, no moccasins, no fun. As for today . . . you can be a watcher.

"Al-vin's a wat-cher," he sang. "Al-vin's a wat-cher."

I didn't want to be a watcher. I wanted to play. But the trouble with Pinky is that he makes all the rules. And usually Rule Number 1 is that I'm not allowed to join in.

"Well, there's only one way to find out if you're going to Hobson's party," said Sam, taking something out of his pocket. It looked like a hairball the size of a fist. Everyone stopped dead in their tracks.

"Sure is ugly," whistled Scooter.

"What is it?" I asked.

"The eyeball of a woolly mammoth," said Sam. "It weighs two pounds."

Everyone gasped.

Sam collects things. Things you'd never laid your eyes on before. Things you never knew existed. And you never know what's going to be in Sam's pockets, especially on Saturdays.

"Where'd you get it?" asked Nhia.

"On vacation," said Sam. He paused. He stroked the eyeball. Then in a hushed voice, he added, "It knows everything. It can see the future."

Everyone leaned in for a closer look.

"Ask it if Alvin will get an invitation," said Eli.

"It can't do anything on an empty stomach," said Sam. "You gotta feed it candy first."

I didn't have any candy, but I had a piece of gum in my pocket. "Here," I said.

Sam popped the gum right into his mouth, chewed, then spat some of the juice into the woolly eye. "Will Alviiiiin get an iiiiiinvitation to the paarty?" Sam asked the eye.

I held my breath.

There was no answer.

"It's crying for candy," said Sam.

Everyone could see that the eye was not crying. There were no tears. But everyone knew where there was a LOT of candy. Eli. Eli's pockets are practically a candy store. And his teeth are ugly to prove it.

So the gang jumped on Eli and cleaned out his pockets. And when it was all laid out on the grass, anyone could tell that there was enough candy to see one hundred years into the future!

After a couple of practice pieces, everyone stuffed their cheeks and got ready. Sam rubbed his giant eye, then we leaned in and spat all at once.

"Mammoth eye," said Sam, drooling heavily, "will Alviiiiin get an iiiiiiiinviiiiiiiiitation?"

Suddenly, the eye started rolling in Sam's hands, slowly at first, then faster and faster! It was terrific! Then Sam dropped it. *Pllluuup!*

"Oops," slurped Sam.

Lucy raced up and put the eye on top of her paws and touched her nose to it in the downward-dog position. Lucy's an expert yoga baller. She can hold her pose until the mammoths thaw.

"What did it say?" I asked.

"It said YYYYYES!" said Sam.

Yes? I didn't hear anything.

"Are you sure?" I asked.

"No," said Sam. "But it'll take some more candy to make sure."

But there was no more candy. We'd eaten the whole store.

And the thing about candy is this. There's LOTS of sugar in it. And when you have that much sugar for breakfast, it makes you go fast-forward like a maniac for no reason at all and you can't stop or rewind.

"*AAAAAAAAAAAAAAAAAAACK!*" I screamed at the top of my lungs, running full speed ahead, clanging on my Firecracker Man helmet.

"*AAAAAAAAAAAAAAAAAAACK!*" screamed the gang, ricocheting around the yard like loose pinballs. No one was playing settlers and Indians anymore, but it was okay. You can wear anything when it's not a war.

That night, after everyone had gone to bed and my brother Calvin was fast asleep, I was still wide awake thinking about what the mammoth eye had said.

YYYYYES!

Yes meant I was going to get an invitation.

My eyes opened wide.

I popped out of bed and rushed over to the window. It was a clear and twinkly night. Up in the sky were so many stars, it looked like someone had spilled them, like Anibelly spilling all her jacks.

"I wish I may, I wish I might," I whispered against the cold glass, "have the first wish I wish upon a star tonight."

"*Grrrrrrrrrrr,*" said Calvin. "*Grrrrrrrrrrrrr.*"

Calvin's a sleep talker. There's no cure for it; it runs in my family. On days when he's done something bad, his entire criminal history will slip out like a greased bicycle chain, just like that.

I listened.

Nothing.

His blankets went up and down.

So I turned back to face the stars.

"I wish . . . ," I began, "I wish . . ."

There were LOTS of stars out, glittering like a million pieces of glass in the street. I could see the Big Dipper and, right above it, the North Star.

"I wish for the Deluxe Indian Chief outfit with fringe," I said, my breath dripping on the glass. "Complete with bow and arrow and the huge feather headdress that makes you look like a giant bird."

I crossed my fingers. It was a big wish. I'd wished for the Deluxe Indian Chief outfit every Christmas and never gotten it. How was I going to get my hands on it now, just so Hobson would invite me to his party?

I didn't know.

"I love you, stars," I added, just in case.

Then I ran and jumped into bed before the flesh-eating critters under it could grab me.

CHAPTER FOUR

Lucky to Be Invited

there was nothing in the mail for me for days.

Then there was something. I could hardly believe it! It was addressed to "Mr. Alvin Ho."

But it was pink.

Invitations to duke it out at a birthday party that was more like a war than a party would not be *pink.*

TV static filled my brain.

I read it out loud:

WHAT: Please come to my
birthday tea party!
WHEN: First Saturday in
November @ 2 pm.
WHERE: My house
WHY: Fun, food, prizes!
HOW: R.S.V.P.
WHO: Flea

Oops.

How could so many stars—and a *hairball*—have gotten it *so wrong*?

"How nice!" said my mom.

Nice? At a boys' party, you duke it out. At a girls' party, you dress up fancy and act strange.

"Tea parties are especially delightful," said my mom. "You'll get to eat finger sandwiches and scones and drink tea."

Finger sandwiches?

I curled my fingers out of sight.

"Do I have to go?" I asked.

"Why wouldn't you want to go, dear?" my mom asked. "Sophie's a good friend to you."

"You mean she's his *girlfriend*," Calvin yelled from the living room. It was after school and he was battling to the death with Anibelly in a video game when he should have been  working on his fourth-grade science fair project.

"She is not!" I shouted.

"Is too!"

"Is not!"

"Is too!"

"Is not!"

"That's enough, boys," said my mom. "Alvin's lucky to be invited."

"That's right," chimed in Anibelly. "Birthday parties are fun."

Birthday parties are scary, especially a *girl's* birthday party. Anything can happen.

You might be dressed for bowling . . .

But everyone else is dressed for swimming.

You could get mistaken for the piñata . . .

Or worse, the donkey for the pin-the-tail game!

Someone might say hello . . .

And expect you to say hello back.

You could break a window.

You could eat too much cake.

You could throw up.

If I had to go to a birthday party, I'd much rather be going to a boys' settlers and Indians party. It would be all-out war with no chance of girls.

"I'll take you shopping, and we can pick out something nice for her," said my mom, smiling. "We haven't done a mom-and-son outing in a long time. Wouldn't that be special?"

Special? I'm allergic to shopping! Whenever we go shopping, my dad and Calvin and I sit like three lobsters in a pot, waiting for the ladies to try on clothes. Why do they have to try on everything anyway? Look at me and Calvin. We don't know what we're going to wear until we get up in the morning and our clothes practically jump on us and we look just fine!

The only good thing about shopping is that if I don't cry too much, I get a treat for being "a patient little gentleman." Usually, I'll pick an ice cream cone, or a new Matchbox car, or an action figure with movable parts.

I blinked.

That's it!

If I agree to go to Flea's party . . .

And I go shopping . . .

And I'm a patient gentleman-in-waiting . . .

I could ask for the Deluxe Indian Chief outfit, instead of an ice cream cone!

And once I get my Deluxe Indian Chief outfit, complete with bow and arrow and the feather headdress that makes you look like a giant bird, Hobson will be sure to invite me to his party!

My heart skipped a beat.

"Okay," I said quickly. "I'll go."

My mom wrapped her soft arms around me and pulled me close. I love it when she does that. I imagined that the deluxe feather headdress wrapping around my head and falling down my back would feel just as nice.

"Alvin's going to a girls' party," I heard Calvin singing from the living room. "Alvin's going to a girls' party."

"Lalalalalalalalala," sang Anibelly.

"Bam! Bam! Bam!" went the video game.

I ran to my room.

I closed the door.

I sifted through the rubble and found my notebook. Then I sat in the golden sunbeam coming through my window and made a list. I didn't want to forget anything.

Things to do:

Go shopping with my mom.
Buy something for Flea.
Get my new deluxe Indian outfit.
Eat breakfast in my new deluxe
    Indian outfit.
Go to school in my new deluxe
Indian outfit.
  Walk down the street in my
new deluxe Indian outfit.
  Sleep in my new deluxe Indian
outfit.
  Play settlers and Indians with
the gang.
  Go to Hobson's party in my new
deluxe Indian outfit.

I stopped. I remembered something I'd heard about girls' parties. *There are always cupcakes.* I love cupcakes. So I added:

Eat cupcakes.

I looked at the pink invitation in my hand. The sun was warm on my back.

Why didn't I get an invitation from Hobson?

I blinked.

A tear plopped onto my list.

Then another.

Then I cried my eyes out.

•–•·•·

Later that night I told Calvin all about the cosmic mistake.

"That's too bad," said Calvin. He was very sympathetic, not like he is during the day when he's wide awake.

"Have you ever been to a girls' party?" I asked.

"Yup," said Calvin. "Twice."

"What's it like?" I asked.

We were tucked in our beds waiting for our dreams to begin. It's the best time to talk to Calvin. He's actually paying attention, like at the cinema when the previews are over and we're just waiting for the real movie to start.

"You get to eat cupcakes," said Calvin.

"What else?"

"There'll be lots of girls," said Calvin.

"What else?"

"The scariest thing is that you have to have special manners," said Calvin.

"Like what?"

"Not really sure," said Calvin. "It's like a secret code or something. You have to know which fork to use for cake and how to pick up the sugar with fancy tweezers, and how to sip your tea with your pinky up and how to hold the saucer thing when you spit it out."

"Oh," I said.

"If you don't know all that," Calvin added solemnly, "they'll ship you out to sea."

Out to sea?

"What else?" I asked.

"You could be the only boy."

"The *only* boy?" I said.

"Yup," said Calvin. "It's a *girls'* party, isn't it?"

I breathed in.

I breathed out.

I didn't feel so good.

"Anything else?" I asked.

Silence.

"Cal?"

The trouble with talking to Calvin when we're both in bed is that he's on very low battery and I'm on AC/DC current. It's a great time to get advice from him, but you have to do it fast. Once he's in shutoff mode, there's no telling whether he's talking to you or talking in his dreams.

"Cal!" I shouted. I turned on my flashlight.

"Yup," said Calvin, turning over.

"How am I ever going to survive a girls' party?" I wailed.

"Hmmmm," said Calvin. "Hmmmmmmmmm-mmmmmmmmmmm."

"Calvin!" I screamed again.

But it was too late. Calvin was fast asleep.

CHAPTER FIVE

Name Tags Are for Neanderthals

if there was anyone who could tell me how to survive a girls' party, it was my cousin Bucky. Her real name is Lizard Breath. She's a girl. She's eight-going-on-eighty-eight, which means she was born with a teacup in her hand and a purse on her elbow. She goes to an all-girls school, which is where no boys are allowed on account of they might ruin things. She just started the third grade but she's already graduated from a special class where she learned all her manners. She even has a certificate on her wall to prove it.

So I ran over to her house after school.

"Bucky!" I rapped on the door of her play-house in her backyard, which is home to Bucky's Veterinarian Hospital and Bucky's Tea House. I could see her through the win-dow. I was in luck. It was teatime. "It's me, Alvin."

"Hi, Alvin!" Bucky waved. "C'mon in."

I went in.

There was scary hospital stuff all over the place: a stethoscope, an otoscope, ham-mers for testing your reflexes, pliers for pulling out teeth, cotton balls, tongue de-pressors and ready-to-go shots on a tray, just like in a real hospital.

My liver flipped.

My head spun.

My eyes closed.

I'm allergic to hospitals. Fortunately, this is an *animal* hospital, and Bucky's pet chinchilla, Chilly, is the only patient. So I slipped into a chair and petted Chilly's soft gray fur until I felt better. Then I opened my eyes.

"For tea came you today says Chilly he's glad," said Bucky, whose words don't always come out in the right order, especially when she's excited. But I understand her perfectly. It's like understanding a foreign language!

"I've been invited to a tea party," I said, pulling the invitation out of my back pocket to show her.

"Oooh," said Bucky. "R.S.V.P. That's French for Resume Standing Very Promptly, you know."

"No," I said. I didn't know.

"You have to do it if you want to go," said Bucky. "It's to tell them you're coming. You can't just show up."

I looked at the certificate on her wall. It was fancy, with a gold seal.

"Calvin says I need to know the special rules, or they'll ship me out to sea!" I said. "Can you teach 'em to me?"

"Sure!" said Bucky. "No problem."

"Do you have any finger sandwiches?" I asked, looking around.

"No," said Bucky.

"Good," I said. "I'm allergic to those."

I looked at the table. Bucky had set it with so many napkins and plates and glasses and forks and cups and spoons that you couldn't see the table.

"Rule Number One," said Bucky. "Show no fear."

"Grrrrrr," I growled. Then I thumped my chest. "Grrrrrrr."

"That's good," said Bucky approvingly.

"Rule Number Two," Bucky continued. "Shake hands and introduce yourself."

I stopped.

"Can't I just wear a name tag?" I asked. "I'd rather wear a name tag."

"No," said Bucky. "Name tags are for Neanderthals."

"Oh, I wish I were a Neanderthal," I sighed. "Or an Indian chief."

Bucky stuck out her gloved hand. She had on a fancy hat, and a little purse swung from her elbow.

"How do you do," she said.

I took her gloved hand and pumped it like an old-fashioned water pump.

"How do you do," I said. I knew what to say

on account of I'd done the handshake before with Bucky. *Many* times before. It's Bucky's thing. But I'd rather wear a name tag.

"That's perfect!" said Bucky, looking very pleased. "Isn't this fun?"

A squeaky sound like the kind Chilly makes when he's unhappy slipped out from me.

"Rule Number Three," said Bucky. "Make eye contact."

"I'm not good at that," I said.

"No problem," said Bucky. "Just practice."

She held a doll up to my face. I made eye contact.

Then she held Chilly up to my face. I made eye contact again.

"See?" she said. "Better you are than you thought."

Bucky was right. I made eye contact, just like that!

"Rule Number Four," Bucky continued. "Drink, eat and talk at the same time. No crumbs allowed."

"How do you do that?" I asked.

"Do like me," she said. She passed me a saltine. Then she took one and popped it into her mouth.

"ChU careFULLWE and SPEEH norMUL," said Bucky. Crumbs shot out of her mouth like water spraying out of a hose. It was great! Then she coughed. *"Hak! Hak!"*

"Into tissue a cough," she said, reaching into her purse and pulling out a wad. "Rule Number Thirty-eight."

"How many rules are there?" I asked.

"Seventy-nine," said Bucky.

Seventy-nine??? My saltine showered like confetti into the air.

"I only need to know about using forks and fancy sugar tweezers and when to spit the tea into my saucer," I said. "Do you know anything about those rules?"

"Yup," said Bucky. "That's lesson two, next week."

"Lesson two?" I said.

"Yup," said Bucky. "The sequel—tableware, utensils and napkins."

"The sequel?"

"Lesson three is dinner conversation.

"Lesson four is how to dress.

"Lesson five is telephone skills and thank-you notes."

Bucky smiled.

"Today's only introductions," she added. "You can't hurry tea."

"But Flea's party is only a few circles away on the calendar," I said. "I can't come for five weeks."

Bucky put down her teapot.

"No problem," she said. "You can do the fast track. Learn all your lessons today."

The fast track? Normally, I'm not a fast tracker. But this was not normal.

"I've got to warn you," said Bucky. "It's ugly."

"Ugly?" I squeaked.

"Tea will spill," said Bucky. "Biscuits will fly."

She picked up her teapot again.

"Ready?" she asked.

"Do I have to drink tea?" I asked.

"No," said Bucky. "There's juice too."

"Okay," I said. "I'll have juice."

Bucky poured, fast.

I looked at what was coming out of her teapot. It was spilling, all right. But it wasn't juice. And it wasn't tea.

"That's just plain water," I said.

Bucky blinked.

"It's *pretend* juice," said Bucky. "Pinky up!"

Bucky sipped quickly and noisily, her pinky up.

I'd barely gotten my pinky up when Bucky barked, "Smile!"

I made fish lips.

"Show no fear!"

"Shake!"

"Put your napkin in your lap!"

"Sit up straight!"

I sat up straight, but I could hardly keep up.

"Time for dim sum!"

"Dim sum!" I said. "I love dim sum!" I was looking forward to flying biscuits, but dim sum was even better! My stomach growled at the thought of it. My mouth watered.

Bucky reached over and put a rock on my plate.

"Dim sum," she said.

"That's not dim sum," I said. "That's dim rock! I can't eat dim rock!"

Bucky looked at it.

Then she looked at me.

"Okay," she said. "Wanna play hospital now? Big old elephant you are and your doctor I am and tooth hurts your. . . ."

CHAPTER SIX

Miracle in a Jar

i was out of Bucky's Tea House and Veterinarian Hospital faster than an earwig out of an ear. When I got home, I told Calvin all about fast-track tea and how scary it got in the end.

Calvin was not really listening to me. He had just come home from karate and was still in a karate mood. He kicked his legs and chopped the air with his hands. "Ha!" he said. "Ha! Ha!"

"What am I going to do?" I asked.

"Ha!" said Calvin. His leg swung over my head.

"I wish I could just disappear," I said.

Calvin stopped.

He looked at me.

"That's it!" said Calvin.

"What's it?" I asked.

"You just gave me an idea for my science fair project!" said Calvin. He ran upstairs. Anibelly and I ran after him. He took out his clipboard and scribbled something.

"What is it, Cal?" I asked.

"Well, if you agree to be my guinea pig," said Calvin, "I can make all your troubles go away."

"Really, Cal?" I asked. Usually Calvin never even lets me *near* his projects. "How?"

"I'll make you invisible," said Calvin. "That way you can go to the party and not be seen. Out of sight . . . out of trouble."

"Hooray!" I cried. My brother Calvin is practically a genius!

"Not so fast," said Calvin. "I'll have to do a bunch of experiments. It might not work at first . . . you might have to be a guinea pig for a while."

"Can I be a guinea pig too?" asked Anibelly. "I've always wanted a guinea pig, but now I can be one!"

"No way," I said. "Calvin said *I'm* the guinea pig."

"You can be a guinea pig too, Anibelly," said Calvin, who always has a good word for Anibelly. "I need to test stuff on more than one person."

"I don't want to test anything," said Anibelly. "I just want to be a guinea pig."

"Great!" said Calvin. "C'mon."

We followed Calvin downstairs, past Gung-Gung, who was supposed to be watching us after school but who had fallen asleep on the couch, straight to the refrigerator.

"If there's anything I've learned in Boy Scouts it's this," said Calvin. "Lemon juice makes good invisible ink."

Calvin took out a bunch of lemons that were already cut up for tea and we squeezed the juice out of them. Then we smeared the juice all over me and Anibelly.

"Lemon juice will make your freckles disappear too," Calvin said to Anibelly. "Want some pulp for extra strength?"

"Yup," she said, "so long as I grow fur and whiskers over 'em like a regular guinea pig." Calvin stuck pulp on the little freckles on her cheeks.

"Extra strength works for me too," I said. I took the lemon peels and stuck them all over myself with duck tape. If there's anything I've learned from my dad it's this: Duck tape is the most useful thing in the house. But I have no idea why it's for the ducks.

Then we waited.

"Are we faded yet?" I asked.

"Nope," said Calvin.

"Are we halfway faded?"

"Nope."

"How 'bout partly faded?"

"Nope."

GungGung stirred on the couch.

"*Oooowwwwooo!*" howled Lucy.

"Lucy says it's time to try something else," said Anibelly.

"Okay," said Calvin.

"Okay," I said. Then we peeled off the lemons, tiptoed past GungGung and hurried back upstairs.

•●•●•

"Miracle in a Jar," said the label on the little jar in my mom's medicine cabinet. "Makes wrinkles disappear overnight. Makes fine lines invisible."

"This may be just the thing," said Calvin, climbing down from the sink. "Do you ever see wrinkles on Mom?"

"No," said Anibelly.

"Do you ever see fine lines?"

"No," I said. "She's just plain. No lines, no tattoos, nothing."

"That's because this cream makes everything disappear," said Calvin. "It's Miracle in a Jar. It's on TV all the time."

Calvin was right. I'd seen it on TV too.

So we rubbed it on. It was cool and felt like whipped butter.

There was only one problem.

There wasn't much cream in that tiny jar. It barely covered two foreheads.

But my mom never runs out of anything. She plans ahead. She buys stuff on sale. So we checked the closet. On a middle shelf, where it was easy to reach, there were quite a few jars of

Miracle in a Jar, next to the extra toilet paper and the extra shampoo and soap.

"It's a good thing Mom's a good shopper," I said.

"If she were a Boy Scout," said Calvin in the quiet voice that he uses when he's turning over a rare baseball card, "she'd make Order of the Arrow."

This time we slathered it on as thick as mayonnaise. The only problem was having to open so many of the little jars just to get enough.

When we finished Anibelly's face, she closed her eyes and smiled peacefully, just like the lady on TV.

When my face was done, I put some on my neck. Then I put the rest in my hair, just in case.

"Lalalalalalalalala," sang Anibelly. She was really happy.

"It's sticky," I said. I was not so happy. "But I can feel it working already," I added.

"Really?" said Calvin. "But the box says it works overnight, and it's not overnight yet."

Anibelly blinked. She looked pretty invisible to me. Only her eyes showed and the little dark holes that were her nostrils.

"It's working!" I screamed. "It's working!"

Calvin looked closely.

Then he stepped back.

Then he stared straight through us.

"This is going to win me the science fair prize," said Calvin, stunned. "I can only see your eyes!"

"Hooray!" I cried.

"Hooray!" cried Anibelly.

I looked in the mirror. I was so covered with Miracle in a Jar that I was practically headless! It was terrific!

So we put away the leftover jars. Calvin said I should use them right before the party.

It was the perfect plan.

My brother was practically a genius!

So I asked him about something else.

"Once I get my Deluxe Indian Chief outfit, Hobson will invite me to his party, won't he?" I asked Calvin.

"Can't be sure about that," said Calvin.

"Why not?"

"Girls will invite you for no good reason,"

said Calvin, "but boys invite you only if you're worth inviting."

"Worth inviting?" I asked.

"You have to either be impressive or do something impressive," said Calvin.

"Like what?"

"Well, for starters, it would help if you got all that cream off your face," said Calvin.

"Okay," I said. I ran to the bathroom and washed off the Miracle in a Jar. Then I ran back to Calvin.

"That's better," said Calvin, inspecting me. "Now you can work on doing something impressive."

"Like what?" I asked.

"Like . . . set a world record," said Calvin.

"A world record?!"

"It has to be an impressive one," said Calvin. "Like . . . most apples split in a minute in midair with a samurai sword. That'll get you invited for sure."

"I can do that!" I said. "No problem!"

I ran downstairs and grabbed an apple from the refrigerator, and then I ran back upstairs.

Then I grabbed Anibelly's gold plastic samurai sword, because I couldn't find my own, and I started to practice.

Whooooooosh! went Anibelly's samurai sword.

Thunk! went the apple on the floor.

Whooooosh! went Anibelly's sword again.

Bonk! went the apple on my head.

"That looks like fun!" said Anibelly, who'd been relaxing on my bed with cream on her face.

"It is!" I said.

"Can I try?" asked Anibelly.

"Sure!" I said.

So then Anibelly set about slicing apples in midair with a samurai sword. It was great fun!

But it was really hard. None of the apples actually got split. They didn't even get thwacked.

Fortunately, I'm good at making lists. So later that night ... after everyone had gone to bed ...

My flashlight was on.

My eyes were wide open.

I opened my notebook.

Next to my old list:

How to Survive a Girls' Party

1. Show no fear.
2. Wear Miracle in a Jar.
3. Don't do fast-track tea.
4. Pinky up!

I began a new list:

WORLD RECORDS
by
Alvin Ho

1. Most apples split in a minute in midair with a samurai sword.

2.

3.

How I was ever going to come up with world records, I had no idea. It was going to be a long, sleepless night.

CHAPTER SEVEN

R.S.V.P.

by the time I got on the bus the next morning, my luck had changed. I was closer than ever to doing something really impressive and getting myself invited to the right party:

WORLD RECORDS
by
Alvin Ho

1. Most apples split in a minute in midair with a samurai sword.

2. Most baseballs pitched into a can in a minute.

3. Most holes dug in a minute with a stick.

4. Most balls juggled in a minute in midair while standing on a chair.

5. Longest hoop shot in the history of the world.

"Wow," said Flea, who was sitting next to me. "I didn't know you could juggle."

I kept my eyes on my page. I didn't know I could juggle either, but it had taken me all night to come up with the list and I wasn't about to start erasing just because I couldn't do something.

"Are you really going to do all that?" asked Flea.

I nodded.

"They look really hard," said Flea.

I nodded again.

"Do you want some help?" asked Flea.

Help? From a girl?

I wanted to say no way, but instead, my head dropped forward unexpectedly and then rolled like a wheel on a roller skate. I was really sleepy.

"Great!" said Flea. "I'll come over after school to help you."

Flea's my desk buddy and she's always trying to help me. It's so annoying.

But going to school without any sleep is the only good reason the buddy system exists.

This is how to use a buddy on a bad day:

Put her in front of you during dodgeball.

Keep her in front of you during dodgeball.

Hold her in front of you during dodgeball.

Piggyback on her going down stairs.

Stick like a static-cling sock on her going through doors (to avoid going through a closed one).

Normally, Flea likes being my buddy. In fact, she volunteered for the job. But today, she squirmed quite a lot and got away from me a few times. In fact, she was acting like a sea captain scraping a barnacle off the side of her boat. I couldn't figure it out. It was a strange way for a buddy to act.

"Miss P," I heard Flea say. "Alvin's acting very strange today."

"Alvin?" said Miss P. "Are you okay?"

I avoided eye contact, which was easy to do

because I could hardly keep my eyes open anyway. I kept my hands in plain sight.

"You look a little pale," Miss P
said. "Do you need to go to the
nurse?"

I kept my head down. I
swung my feet; it was
a sign to show that I
was okay.

Miss P is very smart.
She doesn't need to
hear my voice to know
what I'm saying.

Slowly Miss P turned around and went back
to teaching.

"How do we learn about people living long
ago?" she asked.

"Google them," said Ophelia.

"Watch TV," said Eli.

"Visit their homes," said Sara Jane. "Get the
tour."

"We can also look at old photographs, they
tell us a lot," said Miss P. She dimmed the lights.

She flipped a switch and an old photo flashed on the screen. It was brown and faded in places like an old sneaker. Creepy girls in creepy dresses sat staring at us from a table. I yawned. My eyelids hung low.

"What does this picture tell us?" asked Miss P.

"Girls wore pretty dresses in the old days," said Flea.

"They look like they're about to have a party," said Sara Jane.

"With cupcakes and lemonade," said Esha.

I yawned again. My head felt like a bowling ball about to roll away.

"The title of this photo is 'A Girls' Party,'" said Miss P.

My eyes popped out like peas. THAT'S a GIRLS' PARTY??? Yikes! Everyone looked completely bored to death! No one was even smiling.

"Psssst," said Flea into my ear. "Did you get my invitation?"

I froze.

"You're supposed to Arrrr. Esss. Veee. Peeeeee," said Flea.

R.S.V.P.? What's that? I wanted to ask. But I couldn't. A thousand splinters filled my mouth.

Suddenly I remembered what R.S.V.P. meant. Bucky had told me—it was French for "Resume Standing Very Promptly." You have to do it if you want to go to the party. I didn't really want to go to a creepy girls' party, especially after seeing that photo! But I sure did want to get that Deluxe Indian Chief outfit with all the works . . . and I would be invisible at the party anyway, thanks to Miracle in a Jar . . . so I stood up.

But it didn't feel like I was standing at all. I wobbled this way. Then I wobbled that way. Then I felt my feet leaving the floor, and my body starting to float up, up, up . . .

"Alvin?" I heard Miss P say. "Are you okay?"

A giggle went through the room.

"Pssssst," hissed Flea. "Sit down!"

My butt lowered itself into my seat, like lava in a Lava lamp.

My head turned slowly from left to right, like a summer fan set on LOW.

I could feel Miss P's eyes on me. She's very nice. But she has a habit of keeping her eye on you when you don't want her to.

Fortunately, Miss P did not ask me again if I needed to see the nurse. Instead, she switched off the overhead projector, switched on the lights and switched the subject.

"Diaries," said Miss P, "are another way to learn how people lived."

My eyelids drooped heavily again. I leaned one way in my seat. Then I leaned the other way. It felt like I was on a swing.

"Henry kept a diary," I heard someone say.

"That's right," said Miss P. "Henry Thoreau used to carry a notebook and a notched stick with him on his daily walks."

"Henry wrote about the animals and plants and other things he saw," said another voice.

Then Miss P began to read from Henry's journal. " 'I once set fire to the woods . . . ,' " read Miss P.

I knew that story. Henry and a friend had wanted to catch fish and cook it "Indian-like," in the woods, but they ended up burning down the entire forest!

" 'At the shoemaker's near the river, we obtained a match . . . ,' " Miss P continued. " '. . . The earth was uncommonly dry, and our fire . . . suddenly caught the dry grass. . . .' "

"ZZZZZZzzzzzzzzzzz . . ." I floated up, up, up, out the window, over the school, through the woods . . . until I saw young Henry cooking his catch Indian-like, on the shores of Fair Haven Pond!

"Hey, Henry!" I called out. "I'm going to play Indian too . . . as soon as I get my Deluxe Indian Chief outfit . . . zzzzzzzzz . . . complete with a huge feather headdress . . . as a reward . . . for going shopping and buying something for a *girl*, and then going to the *girl's* scary party . . . where there better be cupcakes! Zzzzzzzzzzz."

"What did you say???" said a voice. Then I felt a hard shove.

I opened my eyes.

It was Flea. She takes Aggression for Girls after school, and was looking at me—aggressively—through her one good eye. She was not happy.

And everyone else was very still, even Miss P.

Had I said something? I didn't think so. I can't talk in school. I can't even grunt or squeak.

Had I fallen asleep?

Uh-oh. Did I mention that sleep talking runs in my family?

What secret could have possibly slipped out?

I had a bad, sinking feeling it was something I should be taking to my grave.

CHAPTER EIGHT

Death by Deep Knee Bends

if ever i had both feet in the grave, it was now.

"Alvin Ho," said Flea when we got off the bus after school. "We need to talk."

Gulp. The gang turned and stared. I clutched my PDK to my chest.

"But I'm going home first to let my mom know where I'll be. Then I'm coming over . . . after I feed my fish . . . and after I practice my Aggression for Girls."

The gang snickered.

I shrank.

Then Flea turned and hurried down the street on her uneven legs.

And I hurried into my house . . . and straight into the bathroom. There's nothing more important than using the bathroom first when you're about to really get it.

Then I ran to find Calvin.

"Calvin," I said, breathless. "What does it mean when a girl says she needs to *talk* to you?"

Silence.

Calvin was at the computer, surfing the Internet as usual, but he should have been working on his science project. And Anibelly was on my bed, reading. Calvin's eyes were glued to the screen, his body frozen except for his mouse finger. And when Calvin's like that, it's hard to get any information out of him.

"C'mon, Cal," I said. "It's an emergency."

"What kind of emergency?" asked Calvin.

"She's coming over right now," I said.

"Then you're dead meat," said Calvin, without taking his eyes off the computer screen.

"Dead meat?" I said.

"It's a secret code," said Calvin. "Girls are not like boys. If a boy wants to kill you, he says, 'I'm going to kill you.' If a girl wants to kill you, she says, 'We need to talk.' That's the code."

I gasped. "Has a girl ever wanted to talk to you?" I asked.

"Yup," said Calvin.

"How come you're still alive?" I asked.

"I vomited," said Calvin.

"Vomited?"

"Lucky for me I had the flu," said Calvin.

Unlucky for me, I didn't have the flu.

But lucky for me, I had . . . MIRACLE IN A JAR! I ran and grabbed the supply.

"Quick, Calvin," I said. "Help me with this!"

"Aren't you saving that?" Calvin asked. "Don't you need to be invisible for the party?"

"But it's an emergency NOW," I said. "Hurry!"

Calvin and I opened the last jars of my mom's face cream, just like that. Then he helped me spackle it all over my face and head and neck.

"Wow!" said Calvin when we were done. "You're completely *headless.*"

I looked in the mirror.

I was a *headless stump.* It was terrific! My head was gone except for two black marbles that were my eyeballs floating in midair, a couple of nostrils and a few tufts of hair, poking like grass out of snow.

I grabbed Anibelly's samurai sword and hurried outside. When Flea sees a headless samurai slicing apples in midair, she'll scuttle away screaming, that's for sure.

• • • • •

Whoooooosh! went Anibelly's samurai sword.

Thwaaaaaack! went the apple.

"*Raaaaaowwww!*" I yelled. "*Raaaaaaaowwww!*"

I was fierce. But the wind
was even fiercer.

"*Ooooooooooo,*" howled
the wind. "*Ooooooooooo.*"

Whoooooooosh!

Thwaaaaaaaaack!

Setting a world record was still
harder than it looked. None of the apples actually split. They just got thwacked.

And there was no sign of Flea.

And it was kind of boring without anyone to
scare . . . or impress.

So I ran back to my room. Calvin was still sitting at the computer and Anibelly was still on
my bed with a book. No one looked up.

So I looked out the window. And there coming up the front walk, finally, was Flea!

"*Eeeeeeeeep!*" I cried.

She was swinging her peg leg as fast as she
could go. Both her legs appeared to get shorter
and shorter the closer she got, until she was di-
rectly under my window, where they disappeared
altogether and I could see only the top of her

head and her pigtails sticking out. It was the perfect target.

I raised the window.

Dingdong! went the doorbell.

I bent over. If I could have vomited an entire watermelon on her, that would have been the end of that. But nothing came out.

"Aaaaaaaalvin!" yelled my gunggung, who was babysitting again. "Someone's here to see you."

I closed the window. I didn't feel so good.

"Coming, GungGung," I yelled.

But I wasn't going anywhere fast.

I took out my PDK.

I put the whistle around my neck.

I tied the bandana for preventing smoke inhalation around my neck.

I put the mirror for signaling (but also good for blinding your enemies) in my pocket, just in case.

I grabbed Anibelly's samurai sword and stopped to admire myself in the mirror. The trouble with invisibility, as everyone knows, is that it doesn't last. One minute you're as hidden as earwax, and the next minute you could be as plain to see as a booger on your lip.

Actually, the booger wasn't on my lip . . . my whole head was a booger! The wind had blown Miracle in a Jar around so much that large patches of my hair were showing and my skin was bare in spots. I pushed the cream around until I was faceless again, but there wasn't enough to make me headless.

So I pulled on my chain mail.

"I thought that was for slaying dragons, not for talking to girls," said Anibelly, who had appeared behind me.

"It's the same thing," I said.

But the problem with chain mail is that it's heavy. And my Roman gladiator outfit with breastplate, shield and helmet, on top of the chain mail, didn't help either.

I looked in the mirror again. I blinked. Who

wouldn't be frightened by a faceless gladiator
samurai knight?

I clanked down the stairs.

Then I clanked into the kitchen.

"Alvin?" said Flea. She was practicing her
Chinese calligraphy with my gunggung, who
likes to teach everyone how to write their Chinese names.

GungGung lifted his brush and peered at me over the tops of his glasses, but said nothing.

"Alvin's going to slay a scary dragon," said Anibelly, who was following me.

"You look pretty scary," said Flea. "I can't see your face at all."

I puffed out my chain mail.

"Grrrrrrr," I growled, remembering Bucky's advice—Show no fear. *"Grrrrrr."*

"Flea said she's here to help you set world records," said my gunggung.

World records?

I thought she wanted to *talk* to me.

Flea held up a mermaid stopwatch and a bag of M&M's.

"What's that for?" I asked.

"You can't set a world record without a stopwatch," said Flea.

"I know that," I said.

"Did you also know that the most M&M's eaten in one minute using chopsticks is thirty-eight?" asked Flea.

"That's a world record?" I said.

"Yup," said Flea.

"I thought world records are supposed to be hard and dangerous," I said.

"They could be fun too," said Flea. "We should do some fun ones first—as a warm-up."

I blinked at Flea.

Then I blinked at her bag of M&M's.

I love M&M's.

"Okay," I said. I didn't want to sound too excited. But inside, I was jumping up and down . . . just like Anibelly.

"Me too?" said Anibelly. "I'm better with chopsticks than Alvin."

"Sure," said Flea.

 So then we all gave it a try, even my gunggung.

M&M's spun and rolled.

Chopsticks clicked and clacked.

It was terrific!

I ate five M&M's. Flea ate three. Anibelly ate six. And my gunggung was terrific—he ate nineteen!

"That's thirty-three between all of us!" said Flea. "We're almost there on the first try!"

I nodded.

Miracle in a Jar tasted horrible.

The insides of my cheeks turned into sandpaper with little pieces of M&M's sticking to them.

I blinked at Flea again.

Then I blinked at the M&M's.

Flea didn't look like she was trying to *talk* to me. So I popped a couple of M&M's into my mouth with my fingers.

Then I turned and ran out the door. Flea and Anibelly and Lucy rushed out close behind. We ran around the yard full speed ahead. Leaves flew. Anibelly squealed. Chain mail shifted. The fall air smelled like rotten apples and Miracle in a Jar.

"Time for deep knee bends," said Flea, catching her breath. "The most deep knee bends done in one minute is fifty-five."

"Watch me," I said. I put down Anibelly's sword. I puffed out my chain mail.

"Me too!" said Anibelly.

"*Owwwwooooo!*" said Lucy. She stretched into her downward-dog pose.

"One . . . two . . . three . . . ," I puffed, going up and down. "Hey, this is SO easy!"

"Yup," said Flea.

"Which would you say is more important," I huffed, "being a scientist or being a world record setter?"

"Well, a scientist can go into outer space," said Flea. "That's pretty important.

"And a record setter . . . ," Flea continued, "shows what can be done if you don't give up. That's super-important."

"You're right," I said, breathless and feeling super-important.

"One, two, buckle my shoe," said Anibelly, also going up and down. "Three, four, shut the door."

"You have to go much faster, Alvin," said Flea. "Like Anibelly."

Oooh. It really curdled my tofu.

So I went faster.

My breath puffed out like car exhaust. The air was cool, but my chain mail was beginning to feel like an electric fence. The gladiator pieces didn't help either. So I took off the gladiator stuff, but I kept the chain mail on, just in case.

I huffed and puffed.

"That's much better," said Flea, clicking her mermaid stopwatch.

"One . . . two . . ." Fireworks exploded inside my brain. "Three . . . six . . ." Flaming swords sliced my thighs. Everything hurt.

"C'mon, Alvin, you can do it!" said Flea. "Faster!"

"Thirty-eight . . . sixty-one . . ." I stopped.

Was Flea still trying to *talk* to me?

Was this *death by deep knee bends*?

My knees locked.

My legs turned into bamboo sticks.

"No, I can't!" I cried. "And you can't make me!"

Flea clicked off her stopwatch.

"Setting world records was your idea," she said.

"I thought you came over to *talk* to me," I said, using the secret code.

"I did," said Flea.

"Do you still want to *talk* to me?" I asked.

"Yup," said Flea. "But I wanted to do something fun first, then talk."

I gasped. Flea was talking in code! Worse, I understood it!

I blinked at Flea. She's from a long line of pirates, and pirates, as everyone knows, are dangerous even if they look like fun.

Leaves swirled all around me.

I didn't feel so good.

"Alvin's going to throw up!" cried Anibelly. "Alvin's going to throw up!"

CHAPTER NINE

Busted

i never did find out what it was that Flea
wanted to talk to me about.

Lucky for me, she left after I threw up.

Then my mom came home.

"AAAAALVIN!" my mom shrieked when she
saw me in the bathroom, where GungGung
had already started the water for my bath.
"WHAAAAT HAPPENED TO YOU?"

She dropped to her knees. She peeled off
my clothes.

"You poor thing," said my mom. "Just look at you!"

My mom is SO sweet.

She took out the biggest, softest towels. She fetched my bathrobe and my slippers. She tested the water. And just as she was about to drop me in the bath, she touched my face.

"What's this on your face?" she asked. "You look like a cake covered in buttercream frosting. . . ."

I blinked.

My mom blinked.

Her mouth opened, but nothing came out.

I don't think I need to tell you how busted I got for using up all my mom's expensive face cream in tiny jars. I got busted so bad that my mom didn't need to kill me, I already wished I were dead. Calvin got busted too; he got grounded from experimenting with anything that belonged to my mom.

Worse, I got even more busted for explaining

that I needed to make myself *headless* to scare Flea, who wanted to *talk* to me.

The look on my mom's face was not good. She definitely needed a Miracle in a Jar.

Then my dad came home.

And we got busted all over again.

"Boys," said my dad. "A gentleman never messes with a lady's things."

"Sorry, Dad," said Calvin.

"Yeah, Dad," I peeped.

"Are you having trouble coming up with a science project?" my dad asked Calvin.

"Kind of," said Calvin.

"Well, come with me," said my dad. "I've got just the remedy for that."

Calvin and I followed my dad out to the garage, where—surprise, surprise—my dad handed over to Calvin an old microscope set, safety goggles and a spiffy white lab coat that said "Junior Scientist" on the chest.

"I had hours of fun with this when I was about your age," said my dad. "Maybe it'll inspire you to do some interesting experiments too . . . and keep you out of trouble."

"Wow," said Calvin. He slipped right into the white lab coat and rolled up his sleeves. "I didn't expect to get a white lab coat," he said.

I blinked.

I hadn't expected Calvin to get a white lab coat either.

Then my dad looked at me.

If Calvin got a prize for getting busted, it looked like I was about to get one too! After all, I needed something spectacular to keep me out of trouble, didn't I?

"Alvin," said my dad.

I stepped closer.

My dad put his hands on my shoulders. He was saving the best for last, I was sure of it. What could be better than a white lab coat? A Deluxe Indian Chief outfit!

I closed my eyes. I could almost feel the head-dress tickling down my back.

"A gentleman would call or go in person to make things right," said my dad. "The sooner the better."

I blinked.

Then I blinked back tears.

That was it? No prize for me?

Calvin hurried off with his loot. Getting busted is the best spectator sport at our house, but when it's over it's over. You don't want to hang around, just in case.

"What's the matter, son?" my dad asked.

I sniffed.

I wiped away a tear.

Through the garage window I could hear Anibelly in the kitchen getting out the pots and pans to help my mom start dinner while singing at the top of her lungs, "Lalalalalalala."

Then it all came gushing out: how scared I was of a girl who wanted to talk to me for no good reason; how I'd made the same girl mad at me, which meant that lightning was going to strike me dead any

minute now. How hard it was to set a world record. How a Deluxe Indian Chief outfit would solve all my problems. How nothing was going right. How everything was falling apart.

My dad listened. He held all my words in his ears. He wiped my tears. Then he held me. We were quiet for a very, very long time.

Then my dad said to me, "I can't help you with most of those problems, son, but maybe I can help you with one."

"Which one, Dad?"

"The most important one," said my dad.

"The most important one?" I sniffed.

"Yup," said my dad, taking my hand in his. I love it when my dad holds my hand. I love it more than anything.

Then we followed Anibelly's singing back into the house.

CHAPTER TEN

How to Talk to a Girl

it was thundering like crazy after dinner.

Lightning filled our windows.

Rain hit our house like a shower of bullets in a video game.

Usually my dad gets it right when he helps me. It's one of his talents. But this time he got it all wrong. He wasn't even close. This wasn't the help that I had in mind:

How to Talk to a Girl

1. Listen with both ears.

2. Look her in the eye.

3. Nod or smile to show that you are doing # 1.

4. Use your indoor voice.

5. Don't scream.

6. Don't carry a concealed weapon.

7. Don't carry a weapon, period.

8. Don't wear a mask.

9. Don't burp.

10. Don't fart.

11. Don't do anything you think might impress her. (See 5-10)

12. Just be yourself.

Then I read it to Calvin.

"You're going to need a lot of practice or you won't even get past hello," said Calvin.

"Hello?" I said.

"You gotta say hello when you're talking on the phone," piped up Anibelly, who was curled up on my bed with a book. "Everyone knows that."

Gulp. Bucky had mentioned telephone skills but we had skipped them on the fast track.

It was homework time, but I didn't have any homework except to practice my handwriting, which I had already done. Calvin was in his white lab coat and should have been working on his science fair project, but instead he was in the bathroom adjusting his safety goggles in the mirror for a very long time.

"Luckily, it doesn't say you can't vomit . . . or carry your PDK," said Calvin. Then he reached into his white lab coat pocket and pulled out a stopwatch.

"Wow," I said. "Did that come with your lab coat?"

"Sure did," said Calvin, showing it off.

"What are you going to do with it?" I asked.

"Something scientific . . . like . . . time the seconds between the lightning and the thunder," he said, running over to the window.

"Can I help?" I asked.

"Nope," said Calvin. "Don't need your help. Besides, don't you need to call that girl and apologize?"

"What girl?"

"If you don't square your crimes," Calvin warned, "THOU ART ONLY MARKED FOR THE HOT VENGEANCE AND THE ROD OF HEAVEN."

I gasped. It was the worst Shakespearean curse in the world! My dad has a whole collection of them in a tin can, and they're all scary, but this one meant I would D-I-E.

"Okay!" I said. "But I need to practice first. Will you help me?"

"I'll help you," said Anibelly, popping off my bed. "I'll be the girl . . . and you call me."

I gripped my list and faced Anibelly.

I blinked.

Anibelly blinked.

"What are you waiting for?" asked Anibelly.

"I don't know what your ring tone is," I said.

"Lalalalalalalala," sang Anibelly.

"*Owwwwooooo!*" sang Lucy.

"Are you sure that's a ring tone?" I asked.

"Just say hello," said Anibelly, tapping her Hokey Pokey toe.

"Hello," I said.

"Hello," said Anibelly cheerfully.

Tick, tick, tick, tick, tick, went Calvin's stopwatch.

"You have to say something after hello," said Anibelly.

I squeezed my eyes shut tight. That's what happens when I'm thinking. My eyes shut. It keeps my thoughts from escaping and getting lost.

But the problem was I didn't have any thoughts. Not one. Only *tick, tick, tick, tick, tick* . . .

I blinked.

"I have to say something?" I asked.

Calvin came over. He wrote something on his clipboard. "It took you two minutes and five seconds to say hello," he said.

"Oh," I said.

"Try it again," said Calvin, "and I'll time you to see if you can do it faster."

Tick, tick, tick, tick . . .

Practicing calling a girl was harder than slicing apples in midair with a samurai sword! I couldn't get past hello.

When I finally got past hello and said, "THIS IS ALVIN!" Calvin said that it took three minutes, forty-nine seconds. He wrote it on his clipboard, like this:

3:49

which was fine. But then Anibelly said that I was too loud, which meant that I broke Rule Number 4, "Use your indoor voice," and Rule Number 5, "Don't scream."

By the time I got past hello and "THIS IS ALVIN!" and said, "I'D LIKE TO SPEAK TO FLEA!" I was wearing a scary mask and twirling Anibelly's samurai sword above my head. How the mask got on my face and how the sword got in my hand, I'll never know. It was a weapon, and it wasn't even concealed, which meant that I'd broken Rules Number 4, 5, 6, 7 and 8, and knocked a few things off the wall, just like that.

"WHAT'S GOING ON UP THERE?" screamed my dad from downstairs. "IT'S A LIGHTNING STORM OUTSIDE, BUT INSIDE, IT SOUNDS LIKE A METEORITE STORM!"

"It's just Alvin, Dad!" screamed Anibelly. "He's practicing how to talk to a girl."

Then something huge exploded outside.

BOOOOOOOOM!

The house rumbled and shook. Calvin scribbled something on his clipboard.

The good news was that I was getting faster, maybe almost as fast as the thunder following the lightning.

The bad news was that I hadn't done it for real yet.

Brrrriiiiiiiiiing. The phone rang.

"AAALVIN . . . TELEPHONE!" my dad shouted from downstairs.

I froze.

Telephone for me?

Gulp.

Who was it? I wanted to ask my dad, but I couldn't. My mouth was already full of wood chips.

So I did the only thing I could do. I picked up the phone in my room.

First, I heard the sound of loud breathing.

I waited.

Then the loud breathing got louder . . . and louder . . .

Until it burst. "HELLO? HEL-LOOOW! ALVIN! ALVIN! ARE YOU THERE, ALVIN?" It was Flea's voice, and it was turned up really loud.

I was there, but I couldn't say so. So I tried Number 1 on the list, "Listen with both ears." I switched the phone from one ear to the other, very fast. It was really hard trying to listen with both ears, but somehow I managed to do it and I heard her say,

"YOU'RE SUPPOSED TO R.S.V.P. FOR MY PARTY!"

But I did R.S.V.P.! I had done it right there in class where she could see me doing it. And if you asked me, I just didn't see how doing it over the phone, where she couldn't see me, would do any good.

I couldn't do Number 2 on the list—"Look her in the eye."

But I could do Number 3—I nodded. Then I made fish lips. It was the best I could do for a smile.

"ALVIN? ALVIN?"

So I Resumed Standing Very Promptly *again.* And I stomped both my feet to prove it.

Oooh. Girls are so annoying. If it weren't for the cupcakes and the Deluxe Indian Chief outfit waiting for me, I never would have agreed to go.

GET THEE OFF THE PHONE DURING

A LIGHTNING STORM, THOU SPLEENY CLAY-BRAINED MEASLE! I wanted to say, but I couldn't. I'd lost my voice. So I clicked the *off* button, and that was the end of that.

Then Calvin wrote on his clipboard:

Phone call
00:14
seconds

CHAPTER ELEVEN

What's the Matter with Alvin?

i was still worried about lightning striking me, making me crispy on the outside and tender on the inside, when I popped out of bed the next morning.

But I wasn't worried for long, on account of it took my clothes 00:05 seconds to jump on me, according to Calvin's scientific stop-watch. Then it took me 00:01 second to notice that there was a police car in our driveway.

It was the best thing that had ever parked in our driveway! I was speechless.

"C'mon, let's go!" Calvin said excitedly.

We hurried downstairs. My mom had already left for work and taken Anibelly to day care, and my dad was in the driveway talking to a policeman.

"What happened, Dad?" asked Calvin.

"Looks like the lightning took out our kitchen tree last night," said my dad.

I gasped.

Sure enough, our kitchen tree, which was also the biggest tree in our yard, was split clean through. Half of it had fallen and smashed a part of the fence into smithereens. The other half was a burnt finger pointing upward at the exact spot in the sky where a finger of lightning had pointed downward to zap it.

Gulp.

Hot vengeance and the rod of Heaven!

"Worst damage I've seen in years," said the policeman, shaking his head. "Normally Concord doesn't attract lightning like that. You're lucky it didn't hit your house, son." He looked me smack in the eye.

Wow. Yellow tape everywhere. The smell of roast tree and wet leaves. A police car in my driveway. A policeman calling me "son." It was a regular crime scene! The gang waiting for the school bus at the bottom of my driveway was staring with their mouths wide open.

And when we got on the bus, there was a hushed silence as I marched up the aisle.

Heads turned.

Seats shifted.

"Man," said Pinky.

"Dude," said Eli.

"Hey," said Scooter.

Normally, none of them says anything to me and all the  seats with the gang are taken and I have to sit with the girls.

But today, things were different. There was a police car in my driveway. It was my lucky day!

I slipped into the seat next to Hobson. He was so impressed by everything that he was still craning his neck to look out the window when the bus pulled away.

Hobson whistled. "Man," he said. "I wish I could get a police car in my driveway."

I swung my feet.

I held up my chin.

Then out of the corner of my eye I saw Flea. She was shooting eye darts in my direction from her non-pirate eye. Then she looked down and began reading a book. I have no idea what that meant. Girls are strange. One day they make all sorts of plans to talk to you, and the next day they ignore you completely.

So I ignored her too. And I pulled out Calvin's stopwatch. It sure was marvelous. Press the green button and the seconds flash by. Press the red button and everything stops.

"What's that for?" asked Hobson.

"You can't set a world record without a stop-watch," I said.

Then I showed him my list:

WORLD RECORDS
by
Alvin Ho

1. Most apples split in a minute in midair with a samurai sword.

2. Most baseballs pitched into a can in a minute.

3. Most holes dug in a minute with a stick.

4. Most balls juggled in a minute in midair while standing on a chair.

5. Longest hoop shot in the history of the world.

"You really gonna do all that?" asked Hobson.

"Yup," I said.

Hobson turned and stared out the window again.

I was *this close* to getting an invitation to his party!

The backpacks on the bus went *thumpity-thump*.

The lunch boxes on the bus went *clickity-clack*.

The _____ on the bus went _____-_____.

Oops. Something was missing . . .

Something that's usually rattling on the bus wasn't rattling . . . it wasn't even there.

What was it?

I scratched my ear.

I picked my nose.

WHERE WAS MY PDK???

"OH NO!" I cried. I was so excited to see the police car in my driveway this morning that I'd forgotten my PDK!

I've *never* gone to school without my PDK!

 "STOP THE BUS!!!" I cried. "TURN AROUND!!! IT'S AN EMERGENCY!!! I FORGOT MY PDK!!!"

But the noise on the bus went round and round.

The fighting on the bus went back and forth.

No one heard me.

No one even turned around.

And our driver, who yells, "SIMMER DOWN OR IT'S STRAIGHT TO THE PRINCIPAL'S OFFICE FOR YOU!" when someone's having an outburst, said nothing.

My head spun.

My saliva dried up.

My liver shriveled.

What was I going to do without my PDK?

Cry.

I bawled full blast. I howled and wailed.

My nose ran like soup.

My eyes puffed out like marshmallows.

Crying is really terrific. Usually everything is better afterwards.

But not this time.

Phooooomp! I tripped coming off the bus.

Swat! A door swung open and flattened me like a fly.

Oooomph! A backpack knocked me over.

By the time I staggered into Miss P's classroom, it was no longer my lucky day.

Miss P took attendance and then she said something about going straightaway to the cafeteria. So I grabbed my lunch box and got into a line behind her and followed everyone down the hall.

When we got to the cafeteria, there was a lot of shuffling and pushing. Kids were standing in long, snaky lines.

"What's the matter with Alvin?" asked Jules as we were standing there.

Heads turned.

"He forgot his PDK," said Nhia.

Silence.

"He doesn't have the right shirt on," said Sam.

More heads turned.

My head turned too . . . and I noticed something funny.

Sam, who usually has a bad hair day, was having a good hair day. A *very* good hair day. His hair was parted on one side and slicked down with gel.

In fact, quite a few of the guys had gel in their hair. And they were all wearing shirts with collars.

And khaki pants, just like the guys who deliver packages.

I didn't know why I hadn't noticed it on the bus.

Or the girls in their nice outfits.

Even Miss P looked different. She had on her best hair, fresh from the beauty parlor. Her shoes were shiny, and her smile was lovelier than usual. She might have even brushed her teeth.

"Miss P," yelled Flea, who's always trying to be helpful. "Alvin needs a shirt."

Miss P rushed over. "Oh, Alvin," she said, bending down to look at me. "Did you forget it was picture day?"

Picture day??? I had no idea it was picture day.

"Don't worry," said Miss P. "After one of the boys gets his picture taken, you can borrow his shirt."

"You can have mine," said Eli as soon as Miss P walked away. Then he took off his shirt and gave it to me, just like that.

But then Eli didn't have a shirt on.

So Nhia said that Eli could borrow his shirt.

Then Nhia was shirtless.

Then Sam tore off his shirt and gave it to Nhia.

Then Sam was shirtless.

This made Scooter rip off his shirt so fast a button went flying. "You can borrow mine," he said to Sam.

"Thanks," said Sam, putting it on and buttoning up the remaining buttons.

Then Scooter was shirtless.

Then Jules said Scooter could borrow his or her shirt as long as Scooter didn't wipe his nose on the sleeve, on account of Scooter had a cold, as anyone could see.

Then Jules was shirtless.

But no one knows for sure whether Jules is a boy or a girl. So then the girls began trading

shirts and dresses and a shirt got passed to Jules, who put it on.

But then Flea was shirtless.

So then I took off my shirt, which wasn't really my shirt, and gave it to Flea. I think it was the gentlemanly thing to do since I hadn't been so nice to her the day before and never did call to apologize. And giving her the shirt off my back, as everyone knows, is a very good apology.

"Thanks, Alvin," said Flea.

"No problem," I said with my eyes. Then I looked at Calvin's stopwatch. It said "00:29," which was probably a world record for borrowing shirts. It was terrific!

But Miss P was not impressed.

And neither was the lady with the camera.

Several of us were shirtless, including me, and it took quite a while for us to get our pictures taken on account of there was a silly new rule that Miss P made up on the spot. If you had a shirt on, you had to keep it on, which meant that only one shirt was passed around to the shirtless and we had to wait our turn. This took 32:54.

Finally, it was time to sit for our big class picture, the one that we would treasure forever, where everyone is in it including our teacher, Miss P, who is very nice.

First there was a mad scramble for shirts.

Then there was a mad shuffling of bodies.

"Tall kids in the back," said the lady with the camera. "Medium kids in the middle. Small kids in the front."

Shuffle, shuffle.

Push, push.

"What's the matter with Alvin?" I heard someone ask when we were all finally in place.

Nothing was the matter with me. Someone was just jealous. I was in the front row holding the sign in my hand that said, "Miss Pestalozzi, Grade 2," which is like holding your prisoner number on your chest.

Then I looked down.

My shirt was kind of weird. There were strange little ribbons on it, and something *frilly*.

Worse, it was PINK.

Oh no! Somehow I was wearing a *girl's* shirt!

If I hadn't forgotten my PDK, none of this would have happened.

My head hung low.

And that's when I saw: I wasn't in a shirt at all—I was in a *dress*!

"Smile," said the lady with the camera.

Then everything went white.

CHAPTER TWELVE

Anything Can Happen at the Mall

time was running out.

It was time to take me shopping for Flea's present after school.

My mom was very talkative in the car.

"You know, Alvin, I can't remember the last time we went out together, just you and me," she said, looking at me in the rearview mirror.

I smiled. I liked being alone with my mom too.

Calvin and Anibelly had gone to the library with my uncle Dennis, who's our babysitter in a pinch, to work on Calvin's science project, and I had my mom all to myself.

"We should do this more often," said my mom, flicking on the radio.

I nodded. I really wanted to be a gentleman to my mom on account of that's what she's used to from my dad, but I didn't know what a gentleman should say when a lady says they should be together more often.

So I said nothing. I didn't want to mess things up.

Then we arrived at the mall.

My mom looked at this.

Then she looked at that.

And she chatted away about this and that . . .

But I said nothing.

The mall is a very scary place.

You know you're in a mall when there's no sun and no moon and no sky, but everything's still brightly lit all the time.

Worse, children get lured away at malls,

which means that they get kidnapped, which means that *aliens* go shopping too.

"Alvin?" said my mom, bending down and taking my hand. "Are you okay?"

I shook my head, but nothing moved.

"Oh dear," said my mom. "You probably need some food."

My mom knows exactly what I need even before I know what I need. And fortunately the food court is the only place in the mall that's not so scary, on account of aliens don't eat, as everyone knows.

"It's very thoughtful of you to come and pick out a present for Sophie," said my mom when we sat down with our snack.

I stuffed fries into my mouth and nodded.

"A gift should say, 'I thought of you,'" said my mom.

I tipped my head to one side. Then I tipped my head to the other. I tried to imagine a baseball bat saying, "I thought of you," to me on my birthday. It would freak me out!

Sometimes my mom says the strangest things.

My mom sipped her tea. Then she took a fry and nibbled it delicately, like a squirrel tasting an acorn.

"Did you have parties when you were a girl?" I asked her.

"Sure," said my mom. "I had all sorts of parties."

"What's a girls' party like?" I asked.

"Well, it's fun, just like any other party," said my mom. "I had tea parties, jigsaw puzzle parties, makeover parties, dim sum parties and, once, a scavenger hunt party. Your gunggung typed out clues and we followed them to find the prizes he had hidden all over the house."

"What's a makeover party?" I asked.

"That's when you do each other's makeup," said my mom.

"Eeew," I said.

"It's not so different from boys putting on war paint," said my mom.

"But boys look great!" I said. "And girls just look stu . . . I mean silly."

"Alviiiin," said my mom.

I had more to find out, and my mom was the perfect person to ask, so I took a big sip of lemonade, stuffed myself with more fries and was getting ready to ask more questions when—I saw something out of the corner of my eye. . . .

I blinked—I could hardly believe it—but there she was, Miss Louisa May Alcott from Orchard House, walking in the flesh, right inside the mall!

She wasn't dressed like she was three hundred years old anymore.

She was dressed like a teenager!

And she was with a couple of other teenage ladies, who—gulp— were the clones!

My eyes popped out like golf balls.

My mouth opened in an O.

I froze. And when you freeze with your eyes and mouth wide open like that, you're just asking for trouble.

Our eyes met.

Then they locked—like four magnets. *Click!*

Then she looked away, but my eyes were stuck following her as she came closer . . . and closer . . .

AAAAAAAAAAAAAAAAAAAAAAACK! I wanted to scream, but nothing came out of my mouth.

And nothing came out of my mom's mouth either. Her lips were moving, but the audio portion of her program was suddenly dead. All I could hear was the laughter of the teenage Louisa May and her clones as they walked past.

"Alvin?" My mom's voice finally came in again. "Are you okay?"

Okay? Can you be okay when you've just

been eye-locked by a dead author who's finally escaped her house where she gives tours and is roaming the mall disguised as a teenager?

•○•○•

By the time my mom dragged my cold, stiff body over to the toy store, she had to read my mind about what to buy.

"Would Sophie like to grow crystals?" she asked.

Silence.

"Would she like a detective kit?"

Silence.

"How 'bout a karaoke kit?"

Silence.

Then my mom dragged me past the dolls and their clothes.

"Maybe she would like a doll?" said my mom.

Silence.

"Hi, Mrs. Ho," said a voice.

It was Pinky.

I was roast duck.

"Hello, Fauntleroy," said my mom, calling Pinky by his real name. "What are you doing here?"

"I'm here with my mom," said Pinky. "We're shopping for a birthday present."

"Are you shopping for Sophie too?" asked my mom.

"Sophie?" asked Pinky. "Who's Sophie?"

Silence.

Pinky looked at me. Then he looked at the dolls on the shelves.

Then he smiled his evil, wicked smile.

"We'd better be on our way," said my mom, dragging me into the next aisle.

I was glad that Pinky didn't follow. Down the next aisle, my mom and I stopped in front of the costumes.

"Now, that's an idea," said my mom. She

reached up and took down a large box. "Sophie likes to dress up, doesn't she? Wouldn't she look absolutely adorable in this?"

I was staring straight into the plastic window of the Deluxe Indian Princess outfit with fringe, complete with baby carrier and explorer map and moccasins.

It wasn't exactly what I had in mind.

It was the girl kit.

And I wanted the boy kit.

"Alvin," said my mom, "I don't understand why you're not cooperating anymore. This was supposed to be fun."

This was supposed to be my Once-in-a-Lifetime Chance to get the Deluxe Indian *Chief* outfit, complete with a huge feather headdress that makes you look like a giant bird!

It was right there on the shelf next to the Deluxe Indian Princesses.

"Buy One, Get Second at Half Price," said the sign.

But it stayed on the shelf.

Meanwhile the Deluxe Indian Princess got tucked under my mom's arm, and I got tucked under the other.

I was missing my Once-in-a-Lifetime Chance.

Forever.

I wanted to cry my eyes out. It's the best thing to do when the thing you wanted most in your life slips away, just like that . . .

And your mom is sweating from dragging you through the mall, and giving you that look that says she should have just ordered something on the Internet.

"Remind me," my mom said breathlessly when we finally got out to the car, "the. next. time. I. want. to. take. you. shopping. that. it. would. be. easier. just. to. go. to. the. gym."

My poor mom.

CHAPTER THIRTEEN

My Life Was Going to the Girls

my life was going to the girls.

This is what happens when you've gone shopping for a girl and everyone has heard about it by the time you get on the bus the next morning.

You sit with the girls.

At recess, you go with the girls.

At lunch, you eat with the girls.

You listen.

You smile (if you can).

You don't burp.

You don't fart.

You talk about fashion.

"What are you wearing to Flea's party tomorrow?" Esha asked Sara Jane between bites of her egg salad on wheat toast.

"My yellow dress," said Sara Jane, "with my yellow purse and my yellow shoes. It's my favorite."

"I have new cowboy boots that I'm going to wear," said Ophelia.

I kept my eyes on my leftover pad thai. I kept my hands in plain sight. I was sitting at their table, but I was not one of them. I was a bootless, dizzy-eyed puttock.

"I'm going to wear my princess outfit," said Flea.

"I'll wear my fancy hat," said Esha.

I stuffed my cheeks full of Goldfish crackers and made a loud CRUNCH.

"How 'bout you, Alvin?" asked Ophelia. "What are you going to wear?"

"Are you coming, Alvin?" asked Flea. "I didn't get an R.S.V.P."

I Resumed Standing Very Promptly once again!

The girls giggled.

Oooh. They really crunch my crackers. I sat back down.

CRUNCH. CRUNCH. CRUNCH.

A man wears steel-toed boots. A man wears work gloves. A man wears war paint. A man wears an enormous feather headdress that makes him look like a giant bird. A man doesn't talk about what he's going to wear. He just wears it. I wanted to say all this, but I couldn't. I was in school, where I can't make a sound except for . . .

CRUNCH. CRUNCH. CRUNCH.

CRUNCH. CRUNCH. CRUNCH.

BUUUUUUUUUURP! Goldfish eyes and Goldfish bones flew out of my mouth. COUGH. AAAAACHUUUUUUUUUUU!!! Orange flecks of unrecognizable fish innards spewed and landed all over the table, on the egg

BURP!!!

salad sandwich, and on cheeks, foreheads and hair.

"Ewwwwww! Eeeeeeek! Gross!" the girls screamed.

Quickly I opened my PDK.

The principal, who was also the lunch monitor, was headed our way. I pulled on my scary mask and my string of garlic and checked my escape route.

"*Aaaaaaaaaaaaaaaaaaaaaaaack!*" screamed the girls again.

"*Brrrrriiiiiiiiiiiiiiiiiiing!*" went the bell, and the entire cafeteria rushed outside for recess using the exact emergency escape route I had in my PDK.

It was a very close call.

• ● • ● •

"You pulled a good one on the girls," said a voice behind me when I got to the monkey bars.

It was Pinky, and the gang was with him.

I said nothing.

I didn't want any trouble.

I hooked my legs over the top bar and dropped into my sleeping-bat position.

"I'm having a party tomorrow," said Hobson. "Be there or don't be there."

His party? Tomorrow? I didn't know what to say.

"It's at two," said Hobson. "Bring me a present or don't come at all."

Really? That was so easy! I didn't have to set a world record after all! All it took was spewing Goldfish innards on the girls!

But there was something else I needed to do tomorrow . . . what was it?

I scratched my bat head with my bat wing.

"Dress as an Indian or don't bother dressing at all," added Hobson.

That's the great thing about boys' parties— you don't waste any time wondering what you're going to wear.

The other great thing is that there's no

R.S.V.P. You get invited, and you go. You don't have to Resume Standing Very Promptly. You can keep hanging upside down.

That was it! R.S.V.P. Flea's party was also tomorrow. At two.

"Let's go," Pinky said to the gang.

Go? Go where?

Wait!!! I wanted to say. But I couldn't. Nothing came out of my little bat mouth.

And the gang was gone, just like that.

But it was okay.

My life wasn't going to the girls! I'd been invited to the right party after all, and now I wouldn't have to go to the wrong one. I could hardly believe it. My wish had come true!

I could hardly wait to tell my mom.

She wouldn't know what to say when I told her I'd like to have more mother-son time at the mall.

Maybe we'd have fries and lemonade again.

Then she'd take me to exchange the Deluxe Indian Princess for the Deluxe Indian Chief outfit and we'd buy something for Hobson. And that would be the end of that.

.•-•-•.

The problem with telling my mom the good news was that my mom wasn't home. My dad was.

So there was quite a lot of explaining to do.

"You see, Dad, I had wished upon the stars for an invitation to a boys' party . . .

"But the stars got it wrong, and I got invited to a girls' party . . .

"And now, finally, I've been invited to the right party. . . ."

My dad looked at me through one eye, then he looked at me through the other eye. He put down his newspaper. He rubbed his quillery chin.

"You have a problem, son," said my dad.

I nodded.

"Getting two invitations is a nice problem to have," said my dad.

I nodded again.

"BUT," said my dad, "you can't go to two parties at once."

"I don't want to go to both," I said. "I just want to go to the right party."

My dad looked at me again. "You're not caught in a dilemma?" he asked.

I looked at my feet. I didn't know what a dilemma was, but it didn't look like I was caught in anything, so I shook my head no.

"Then you're a better man than I was at your age," said my dad.

"You were a *man* at my age, Dad?" I asked.

"It's an expression," said my dad. "It means you know the right thing to do and you do it. No one has to tell you."

I nodded.

"It's moments like this that make me feel

proud to be your father," said my dad, giving me a pat on the back.

I looked at my dad. He had been working a lot lately and I'd hardly seen him at all.

So I gave him a hug.

And he hugged me back.

Then I said it back to him, "I'm proud to be your son, Dad."

CHAPTER FOURTEEN

Make It Do

i popped out of bed the next morning before anyone else was awake and started putting together my BPDK (Birthday Party Disaster Kit).

You can put anything in a BPDK, but mostly it should be things that are useful at a party.

I wrote "BPDK" on a rolling suitcase, and I put in the following:

Name sticker. Better than shaking hands. Also useful for identifying your body in the event of a fire.

 Permanent marker. For writing your name on the above sticker. Also useful for making a few bucks at a party by doing face-painting and tattoos.

 Party hat.

 Noisemaker.

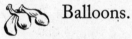 Balloons.

 Fire extinguisher. For the birthday candles.

 Bandana. For preventing smoke inhalation.

 Rope. For escaping out of a second-floor window in case the flames and smoke have gotten out of hand. Also useful for tying up someone who is winning all the games.

A shopping bag. For goodies and party favors.

Then I picked up my list, "How to Talk to a Girl." I stopped.

"'Show No Fear,'" I added to the bottom, remembering Bucky's advice. Then I threw it into my BPDK, just in case.

"Calvin," I whispered. "Could I borrow your Houdini straitjacket?"

Calvin turned over. "Grrrrrrrrrrr," he growled. "Grrrrrrrrrrrr."

It sure sounded like he said, "Go ahead, go ahead."

"Thanks, Cal," I said. Then I picked up his fantastic straitjacket off the floor and stuffed it into the Deluxe Indian Princess box, which I had emptied. It fit perfectly.

Another problem with going to a party is that you should be appropriately dressed. This means that you should dress like everyone else at the party. This is especially scary if you're going to a girls' party.

Lucky for me, I'd already been *told* what to wear.

I didn't have the exact outfit I needed, but it was close enough.

"Use it up, wear it out, make it do or do without," I rapped softly as I stood in front of the mirror. It's one of my dad's favorite sayings. It means don't waste anything. Use whatever you have.

It's good advice.

I turned this way. Then I turned that way. The sun peeped over my shoulder.

The Deluxe Indian Princess outfit didn't look too bad on me. In fact, the longer I looked in the mirror, the less it looked like the Deluxe Indian Princess and more like the Deluxe Indian Chief.

Even the deluxe baby carrier looked like it was meant for carrying arrows, not a doll.

The only thing missing was the huge feather headdress that makes you look like a giant bird. If I had one of those, my outfit would be perfect!

Could I make one?

What would my gunggung do? He makes everything from scratch, even our Halloween costumes.

So I scratched around. And this is what I found: buttons, ribbons, glue and one hundred Popsicle sticks. It was perfect!

.•.•.

By the time I smelled eggs and bacon coming from the kitchen and heard Anibelly singing at the top of her lungs, I was hardly recognizable.

Looking back at me from the mirror was no Indian princess.

It wasn't even Alvin Ho.

It was the best-looking Deluxe Indian Chief I'd ever seen!

"Wow," I said to the mirror breathlessly.

I wanted to rush downstairs and eat breakfast in my amazing new outfit, then run and scream around the yard and dig holes. But I knew I couldn't. The problem with dressing for a party is that you're not supposed to do it until the very last minute on account of you can ruin it all before the party even starts.

So I took everything off, folded it neatly and put it on top of my pillow.

Calvin turned over in his bed. He doesn't pop out like I do. I have alarm clock noise phobia so I'm always up before the alarm goes off, but Calvin always waits for the BEEEEP—BEEEEP—BEEEEEP!

"Rise and shine!" I yelled at Calvin. "I've been up for hours!"

Calvin groaned.

"THOU ART A VERY RAGGED WART!" I screamed, jumping on his bed.

Calvin lifted an eyelid. But he still did not move.

"Thine horrid image doth unfix my hair!" he said. Then, suddenly throwing back

the covers, Calvin screamed, "TRULY THOU ART DOOMED, LIKE AN ILL-ROASTED EGG, ALL ON ONE SIDE!"

Calvin lunged at me.

But I'd been up for hours and was more awake than a ragged wart, so he missed.

Then he chased me down to breakfast.

CHAPTER FIFTEEN

Do Certain Foods Produce More Gas than Others?

saturday mornings are crazy at our house.

Even before breakfast was over, my dad was on the phone calling for a babysitter. He was taking my mom to a QRDO (quiet romantic dinner out) in the evening. None of my grandparents could come watch us and neither could my uncle Dennis.

My mom was busy too. She was making a grocery list and checking the refrigerator and cupboards.

Calvin was in his white lab coat. He had finally settled on a science project that Uncle Dennis suggested and he was working on it at the kitchen table. And Anibelly, Lucy and I were hanging out, watching Saturday-morning cartoons and multitasking—Anibelly was waiting for Calvin to turn her into a guinea pig, Lucy was doing her yoga ball routine, and I was busy wrapping my present for the party.

"Broccoli," said Calvin. "Would you get me broccoli, Mom?"

My mom scribbled it on her list.

"Cauliflower too," Calvin added. "And cabbage."

My mom scribbled. Then she stopped. She looked at Calvin.

"Also green peppers and onions," said Calvin.

My mom's eyes grew big and

round. "Whatever happened to candy, potato chips and ice cream?" she asked.

"Those too," said Calvin. "The vegetables are for my science project."

"I hope it requires you to eat them," said my mom.

"It does," said Calvin.

"Great!" said my mom. "My kind of science project."

Then my mom looked at me. "Any requests from you, Alvin?"

I shook my head. "I like everything," I said. It's true. I eat whatever's in front of me. I'm not a picky eater like Calvin.

"I like everything too!" said Anibelly.

"Are you ready for your party, sweetheart?" my mom asked me.

"Yup," I said. "I can't wait!"

"That's a big change coming from you," said my mom.

"Yup," I said. "I had a talk with Dad."

My mom nodded. "I'm glad you did," she said, smiling at me.

I smiled back. I love my mom.

"He's even got his outfit laid out on his bed," said Calvin.

My mom looked very pleased.

"Alvin," said my mom, "sometimes you really surprise me."

I nodded. "Sometimes I really surprise me too," I said.

"And that's a good wrapping job, by the way," my mom added, going out the door. "If I were the birthday girl, I'd be very happy to receive it."

My chest filled like a large hot-air balloon and I floated up, up, up above my house. If my mom were the birthday girl, I'd give her a hundred and thirty-two kisses.

• • • • •

"Do Certain Foods Produce More Gas than Others?" Calvin wrote across the top of his display board.

"What does that mean?" I asked.

"For this experiment you'll eat different foods," said Calvin. "And we'll see which ones give you the most gas."

"What foods?" I asked.

"The ones I asked Mom to get," said Calvin. "Broccoli, cauliflower, onions, cabbage, green peppers. We already have baked beans. And if you're lactose intolerant like Dad, there's milk, cheese, yogurt, and ice cream."

"Ice cream?" I screamed. "I love ice cream! When do I start?"

"Right now," said Calvin. "Today is ice cream day. Tomorrow will be broccoli day, and the day after that cauliflower day, and so on."

"Hooray!" I said.

"Hooray!" said Anibelly.

"*Oooowwwoooo!*" cried Lucy. She loves ice cream too, especially when she can lick it off of Anibelly.

We hurried to the freezer.

Calvin is a regular backhoe when it comes to scooping out ice cream. Someday he'll work in an ice cream shop. He's very talented in that way.

"Calvin," I said, "you're going to be the best ice cream scooper in Concord."

"Yup," said Calvin, making himself a hill of Dubble Trubble Chocolate Rubble. "But for today, I'm just going to be a guinea pig like you and Anibelly."

"I love science," I said, shoveling Mint Chocolate Cookie into my cheeks.

"Me too," said Calvin.

"Is this going to turn me furry?" asked Anibelly.

"I can't wait for baked bean day," I said.

"I don't like baked beans," said Calvin. "They're too sweet and slimy. But they do give you the most gas."

"Bombs," I said.

"Real bombs," said Calvin. "Like the kind that blew up Concord in the old days."

I laughed.

Calvin laughed.

My brother Calvin's really great. He's usually running around from karate lessons to baseball practice to Boy Scouts to something else. He does it all, which means he's rarely in a talking mood. But when he's in a talking mood, it's like talking to my best friend.

"You're going to be the greatest scientist in the world someday," I said, slurping my ice cream.

"Yup," said Calvin, also slurping. "I'll build a spaceship and blast you off to the moons of Jupiter."

"Can you put a tractor there too?" I asked. "I'd like to ride a tractor out there."

"Sure," said Calvin. *SLUUUURP!*

"And I just want to be a guinea pig," said Anibelly.

"*BUUUUUUUUUUUUUURP!*" I replied.

BUUUUUUUUURP

CHAPTER SIXTEEN

Half-Naked

i got dressed and ready to go, all by myself.

"Wow," said Anibelly.

"Thou hath more feathers than wit!" said Calvin.

"Lalalalalalala," sang Anibelly, dancing around me. It made me feel like dancing too. So I did.

Then it was time for me to leave. I grabbed my present and my BPDK and headed downstairs.

Too bad my dad was underneath his car in the garage and my mom wasn't home from shopping yet. If they had seen me, they would have taken pictures.

"Don't stop along the way," my dad called out to me from underneath his car, Louise. "And come home promptly. Your mother and I are going out and you need to meet the new babysitter when she gets here."

"Okay, Dad!" I shouted, running around the back to inspect our kitchen tree.

Then I climbed into our apple tree.

Then I dug a couple of holes.

After that, I went to see an eagles' nest in a neighbor's yard, but when I got there, it was too far up (I have acrophobia), so I went to the little pond instead, where you could see a family of swans and turtle eggs and not have to climb anything.

An Indian chief's got a lot to do!

"Hey, Alvin!" someone called as soon as I reached Mildred Circle.

It was Sam. The gang was dressed up and playing settlers and Indians right there in the cul-de-sac.

"You heading over to Hobson's party?" asked Eli.

I nodded.

"It's too early," said Pinky. "So we're practicing before we go."

I shrugged. I hopped on my invisible horse and galloped around the circle with my present under my arm, pulling my BPDK behind me.

"Cool outfit," Nhia called out, shooting an invisible arrow at me.

I ducked. Then I gave a loud whoop.

Loud whoops went round and round.

Invisible arrows went up and down.

Indians fell.

Settlers fell.

Indians rose from the dead.

Settlers rose from the dead.

Loud whoops went round and round.

It was terrific!

Then I stopped.

I could hear my dad's voice in my ears. "You know the right thing to do and you do it. No one has to tell you."

I looked around. My dad wasn't there.

Then I heard him again. "You're a better man than I was at your age," said my dad's voice.

I looked around again.

"What's the matter?" asked Jules.

"Nothing," I said.

I began to gallop again.

I could hardly believe it. I was finally on my way to the right party. I was in my Deluxe Indian outfit. I was playing settlers and Indians with the gang. I was impressive.

But it didn't feel like what I had expected.

I stopped again.

"Did you forget your PDK?" asked Pinky.

I shook my head no.

"What's the matter, then?" asked Nhia.

"Maybe I'm not supposed to be here," I said.

"Why not?" asked Nhia.

"Not sure," I said.

I started to gallop again.

Wearing a Deluxe Indian outfit was fabulous!

Playing settlers and Indians was great!

The Popsicle-stick-feather headdress falling down my back was spectacular!

I loved it all.

So why didn't I feel wonderful?

I stopped dead in my horse tracks again.

"My bones are marrowless and my blood is cold," I cried.

Everyone stopped dead in their tracks.

"Is that one of your dad's curses?" asked Sam.

"Waaaaaaaaaaaah!" I cried. *"Waaaaaaaaah!"*

Crying is really great. If you're about to lose it all, you should cry.

"I think I have to be somewhere else," I said at last.

"Where?" asked Sam.

"At that girl's party?" asked Eli.

I nodded.

Eyes shifted.

Legs shifted.

"You're weird," said Pinky.

I felt weird. The more I thought about going to Hobson's party, the stranger I felt. And the more I thought about going to Flea's party, the happier I felt.

I knew what was the right thing to do. My dad was right. No one had to tell me.

But I was not dressed for sipping tea. I was dressed to kill.

Worse, I was wearing Flea's present!

There was only one thing to do. I unwrapped the present I had under my arm.

"Deluxe Indian Princess," it said on the box.

But you could see through the plastic windows that it was not the Deluxe Indian Princess, so I dumped it out.

Then I took off the Deluxe Indian Princess outfit and the deluxe baby carrier that was now a deluxe ammunition carrier, and put them back in the box.

Then I rewrapped the box as best as I could. It looked like origami gone bad.

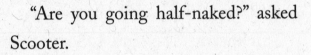

"Are you going half-naked?" asked Scooter.

Oops.

A man can be half-naked when he's on the beach.

A man can be half-naked when he's digging holes.

But a man can't be half-naked going to a party. Everyone knows that.

So I picked up what I had dumped from the box—it was going to be Hobson's present, he would have liked it—and I pulled it over my head.

A man's gotta wear what a man's gotta wear.

And a man doesn't talk about what he wears. He just wears it.

I twirled one sleeve of the straitjacket around the box under my arm, and tied the other sleeve to my BPDK. Then I marched . . . right out of Mildred Circle and straight to Flea's house.

·•·•·

Going to a girls' party was extremely scary.

"Hi, Alvin," said Flea at the door. She looked very surprised to see me.

"Hello, My Name Is Alvin," said my name tag.

Silence.

I'd gotten lots of advice about what to do next, but I couldn't remember any of it, not one word.

Fortunately, it was okay. Flea didn't ask for any more R.S.V.P.s, she just asked me to come in.

There was a piñata.

There was pin-the-tail-on-the-donkey.

There were finger sandwiches (without any fingers).

There were scones.

And lots of cups of punch.

There were girls. Lots and lots of girls.

And Calvin was right.

I was the *only* boy.

Poor me.

But actually, it wasn't that bad.

"This is Alvin," said Flea, introducing me to her friends who didn't go to our school. "He's an Indian chief. He was nearly struck dead by lightning this week."

There were gasps.

"He came *this close* to being split wide open," said Flea. "If it hadn't been for the tree in his yard that took the hit."

Jaws dropped.

"He's also a world-record setter," said Flea. "He can eat five M&M's in a minute with chopsticks!"

There were oohs and aahs.

"He can also do deep knee bends and slice apples in midair with a samurai sword, almost," Flea added.

"What's that he's wearing?" asked a girl whose name sticker said "Bunny." She looked like a little bunny too. Her nose was tiny and pink.

"It's a straitjacket," said Flea. "Alvin is a member of the Houdini Society of Do-It-Yourself Escape People. You can tie him up and put him in a box and he'll escape," she bragged. "Maybe he'll show us."

The girls giggled.

Lucky for me, Flea didn't have a box big enough.

But unlucky for me, there I was, in front of a bunch of girls waiting for me to escape from my straitjacket.

A hush filled the house.

All eyes were on me.

I wiggled this way.

Then I wiggled that way.

I tried to remember how Houdini did it in his video. It didn't take him long . . . it was all going to be over in a minute . . .

Then I exploded.

Like a bomb.

Oops.

Then I exploded again.

It was the ice cream.

And it was not a very gentlemanly thing to do.

"Euuuwwwww!" screamed Flea.

"Grosssss!" screamed the girls.

Pa—pa—pa—pa—pa—pa! I sounded like a machine gun.

Cupcake flew out of my mouth.

Sssssssssssssssssssssss! It sounded like a slow leak from a balloon.

I couldn't help it.

I don't need to tell you how quickly I went home after that.

I didn't even stay for the chicken dance.

·•·•·

It was gas propulsion all the way home.

I was a cannonball that shot across Concord and landed on Calvin when I burst in the door.

My dad was all dressed up and about to have a QRDO with my mom, and my mom looked as beautiful as the Milky Way.

Boooom! I exploded.

"Alvin," said my dad, waving away the smell,

"you're going to have to learn to eat ice cream only when you're safe at home."

"I'm glad you had a good time at Sophie's party," said my mom.

"Me too, Mom," I said.

"Under the circumstances, it was gentlemanly of you to leave," said my mom.

My dad gave me a pat on the back.

Then the doorbell rang. It was our new babysitter.

"Thanks so much for coming," said my mom, greeting her at the door. "I hope the kids will be good for you."

She stepped in. I froze and one last piece of cupcake fell out of my mouth—it was Louisa May Alcott!

Alvin Ho's Creepy Glossary

Abe Lincoln—A super-duper tall guy in a tall hat, with a beard. He was also a President. He signed a law that freed the slaves.

Abolition—The end of slavery.

acrophobia—Fear of being anywhere higher than your tiptoes.

Aggression for Girls—A class that teaches girls how to beat up boys for no good reason.

American Revolutionary War—Battle between Revolutionaries (the colonists) and the Redcoats (the British army). It lasted a long time, from 1775 until 1783. In the end, the British went home and the American colonies became a new country.

BRB—Be Right Back!

Bucky—(1) A girl. (2) Also my cousin. (3) Real name is Lizard Breath. She goes to an all-girls school where no boys are allowed on account of they might ruin things.

chain mail—Originally made to be a fence, but has been worn as clothing since about the time when people started beating up one another with metal weapons. Very heavy. You can't run when you have it on.

deep knee bends—Painful exercise that makes your legs feel like they're on fire and makes you huff and puff like crazy.

earwig—A very scary-looking insect that crawls very fast. People used to believe that they enter the ears of a sleeping person and bore into the brain. I still believe it.

Fair Haven Pond—A great fishing spot in Concord!

fast track—A very scary way to learn something very fast. It's like driving in the passing lane.

Godzilla—Japanese giant monster from the sea who stomped through the streets of Tokyo and made people run and scream like crazy.

Henry David Thoreau—Famous dead author who liked the woods and writing in his journal.

King Philip's War—Started in 1675 in Plymouth Colony, before it became a part of Massachusetts Bay Colony. The war spread and nearly wiped out all of New England in a little more than a year. King Philip was the English name for the Native leader Metacom. The settlers were fighting to take more land away from the Natives and the Natives were fighting to preserve their traditional way of life.

lactose intolerant—My dad. And maybe me too. It has something to do with making a certain kind of noise after eating something made with milk or cheese.

Louisa May Alcott—(1) A famous dead author who wrote *Little Women*. But maybe she wasn't dead when she wrote it, I'm not sure. I can't remember. In fact, I can't remember anything from the tour of her house. (2) Babysits for extra money.

malaria—A deadly disease given to people by mosquitoes. In some countries so many people are sick with it that hardly anyone is able to go to work or school.

Minutemen—A small handpicked force of the Massachusetts militia, who were "ready in a minute." They were the first to arrive at a battle during the American Revolutionary War.

Miracle in a Jar—(1) Comes in tiny jars. (2) Feels like butter. (3) Aka vanishing cream. (4) Expensive.

Neanderthal—Mostly European guys and some Asian ones too, who were hanging out while the Earth was still cooling. Their children had heads as big as our grown-up ones now, and their grown-up heads were the size of XXXL boxing gloves. They were also very strong. They took Aggression for Everybody.

Old Hill Burying Ground—(1) The oldest cemetery in Concord. (2) Next to St. Bernard's Church. (3) The gate is right next to the last house. (4) Don't go there.

Orchard House—(1) Home of the Alcotts. (2) A popular field trip destination. (3) But not a favorite destination of mine, even though it has a cool gift shop.

QRDO—Quiet Romantic Dinner Out. It's NICE for those going out, but STRESSFUL for those staying in with a creepy babysitter.

Ralph Waldo Emerson—(1) A famous dead author who was only leading tours of his house, but is now working a new gig at the cemetery. (2) Reads minds. (3) Is very creepy.

Redcoats—Soldiers of the British Army during the American Revolutionary War. Red was the color of their uniform. Also known as Lobster-backs.

R.S.V.P.—Resume Standing Very Promptly. This is what you do when you get invited to a party and you want to let them know that you're coming. It's French, but it sounds like English to me.

Sam Staples—Concord's tax collector and jail keeper. When he asked Henry Thoreau to pay up his poll tax that he hadn't paid for several years,

Henry volunteered to go to jail instead on account of he didn't want his money to support a government that admitted Texas as a slave state.

samurai sword—(1) A Japanese weapon used by brave warriors called samurai. (2) Also used by Anibelly for bushwhacking, and useful for slicing apples in midair. (3) Plastic. (4) Made in China.

Show No Fear—The best thing to do when talking to a girl.

slavery—This is when one human being says that another belongs to him and has no freedom. First time it occurred in Concord was in 1708. About twelve Concord families owned slaves on the eve of the American Revolution. Places named for slaves that are in Concord today include Jennie Dugan Road, Jennie Dugan Spring, Brister's Hill Road and Peter Spring Road—all named for slaves who, after gaining their freedom, settled in these parts of town.

Sleepy Hollow Cemetery—Huge cemetery full of creepy dead people. Authors' Ridge is at the top of the hill in the back, where all the famous dead authors have tombstones next to one another, but as everyone knows, they're still in town giving tours of their houses. Don't go there.

spackle—It's a kind of putty used to fill holes in walls. You have to smear it on the wall like face cream. So putting on face cream is like spackling.

Underground Railroad—A secret network of brave people who helped runaway slaves in the United States escape to freedom in Canada.

woolly mammoth—Aka *Mammuthus primigenius* and the tundra mammoth. Looks like a huge hairy elephant. Lived about 10,000 years ago, but you can still see them in museums and buy woolly mammoth souvenirs made in China.

world records—When you're the only one in the world to do something special like bend at the knees a hundred times without falling over dead, then you have set a world record.